Copyright © 201_ _____ _____
All rights reserved.

No part of this publication may be reproduced, distributed, or transmitted in any form or by any means, including photocopying, recording, or other electronic or mechanical methods, without the prior written permission of the publisher, except in the case of brief quotations embodied in critical reviews and certain other non-commercial uses permitted by copyright law.

For permission requests, write to the publisher, addressed "Attention: Permissions to Copy," via the website below.

www.reddragontales.com

DEDICATION

I would like to dedicate this final book to Katherine. From the age of two we have been friends and you have shared my passion for all things spooky. We have shared ghost stories as children during sleepovers, learned tarot and dabbled with the Ouija together and today we still actively investigate haunted locations in-between crying, laughing, drinking prosecco and slagging off work, men and life! For being truly the best friend there is. For being so encouraging and enthusiastic about my stories. For always knowing the right things to say and for being a true soul mate x

Thank you.

DEAD HAUNTED 1

By Claire Barrand

To Helen,

Love from

Claire

x ♡

BLEAK MOON

Mary Parry had been feeling in high spirits earlier that May evening, as she had walked along the towpath towards Llandu, taking in and enjoying the last of the warm sunshine. Humming to herself, she had worn her prettiest dress. A crisp white pinafore smartly tied around a blue smock.

Mary was a pretty girl with fair sun-kissed skin and hair streaked with gold and copper. Her green hazel eyes picked up accents of the gold and sparkled brightly.

She felt in her pocket the curious crisp note.

Meet me Upper Yard Bridge at sunset.

Thomas

A flutter in her stomach dared her to hope. She permitted herself to imagine a small wedding at Llandu Chapel, and she could barely contain her anticipation. The fears of the past few weeks felt like they were about to be lifted.

Thomas was the head groom at the hunt stables, and he had promised faithfully they would soon announce their engagement.

It was not, however, wise to be meeting Thomas without a chaperone. Despite her age of 21 years, the villagers would gossip so she had taken her basket to collect flowers for pressing, something she often did.

Mary took great pleasure and pride in gathering wildflowers such as Canterbury Bells and Wild Poppies. She would carefully press them in her scrapbook, tokens and memoirs of illicit meetings with her Thomas. Her passion for him besieged her.

They would meet when he walked the ponies along the canal where he would tie them up, and they would seize precious time together watching the sun go down. Reading poetry together, talking, laughing, and making love.

"*Love...*" she whispered softly to herself as she looked down and tenderly touched the swelling beneath her pinafore.

She had been in despair in the recent weeks after discovering her condition. Mary's father was a strict man. However, he was respected as a hard-working farrier in the village and she, being the eldest of five girls, risked bringing her entire family into disrepute.

The alternative was too horrifying to consider.

To bear an illegitimate child in 1897 would almost certainly see any girl outcast from her family. Unmarried mothers found themselves objects of vicious gossip and scandal, their bastard children born into a life of poverty, cruelty, and abuse, filling up the workhouses, for there were no alternatives, and all deserved in the eyes of society.

Nancy Price, from Gildewi, had born a son last year outside of wedlock. The image was burned into her mind of the village women spitting venom as pitiful Nancy passed them in the street.

The infant was said to have been sickly and had died shortly after birth, and Nancy was sent to live with her Aunt in London.

"The devil's work cannot be undone!" her mother had remarked at the time. The harsh words resonated now in her mind.

Thomas was waiting on the stone bridge that reached over the still water below. A tall, slender young man in his early twenties, he was a dark, brooding figure in his tweed overcoat and long leather boots. He was leaning on the bridge wall staring down at his reflection below.

He did not look up as Mary advanced.

Approaching him, she noted how the sun was gifting his glossy black hair a beautiful halo of light. She picked up the pace, her strained face allowing a tender smile to materialise.

"Thomas!" she breathed, noting at once the happiness in her expression was not shared.

His face was sapped, and his eyes did not meet hers. At once she took his hands.

"Oh, Thomas, Tell me what is troubling you? My love, you look quite ill?"

The unease in her voice was causing it to falter, and as he pulled his hands away from her grasp, he stepped backwards and shook his head.

"No. Nothing is wrong. I asked you to meet me so that I could deliver some news..."

Wavering, he allowed himself a fleeting look at her, but if there were sentiment behind his eyes, it did not show.

"I am to marry. I am engaged to Miss Cynthia Jones of Newport. The arrangements have all been made, I leave next week."

He babbled as if he might choke on the words if he stopped to take a breath.

Thomas had enjoyed his clandestine meetings with the pretty young Mary in recent weeks. It had kept him entertained for the summer months, at any rate. It had satisfied his desires. Yes, their lust fuelled moments in the long grass had ensured his behaviour was impeccable for his arranged meetings with the prosperous landowner and racehorse enthusiast Squire Gordon Jones and his frosty, but wealthy, daughter Cynthia.

The stunned silence between them in this present moment though was transient and from deep inside Mary's gut a yielding wail twisted into a nauseating scream.

"No! Thomas NO! Do you not love me? I have given myself to you my darling... Please? Please, I BEG you..!"

Mary wept as she fell to her knees sobbing.

As she looked up at Thomas pleading with her eyes, she whispered already sensing the hopelessness.

 "I am in a certain condition, you must know...?"

She begged for a reaction, but Thomas backed away

While making a desperate grapple, she tried to stop him but fell flat on her face as he cruelly kicked his leg backwards out of her grasp.

Thomas looked at the wretched girl kneeling before him, muddied, trembling, and sobbing but allowed himself no response. He weakly muttered something inaudible as he turned and walked away, his figure dissolving into the looming shadows of the dusk now closing in on the canal.

Mary watched silently as he grew smaller and smaller, not once did he turn to look back at her.

The flowers in her basket were wilting now...devoid of the life force they sucked through their roots to their delicate stems from the earth. They withered, and the damp smell of decay was already manifesting under the setting sun.

Hours passed.

Her face was now washed clean of tears.

A beam of light from the night sky bounced off the murky soundless water like torchlight. It cast highlights upon long golden hair swaying gently around trying to escape the swollen white flesh. Lifeless eyes, fringed with the thickest lashes. Her pupils were black as the night sky itself, yet the white of her clothes dazzled back in rivalling luminosity.

Her soft hands still cradled her belly, not stirring as fairy fern crept up over her.

The moon, magnanimous and tender, radiated down and its glistening white light reached out kissing her stone cold cheeks and liberating from its depths, two hopeless souls.

Months passed, and Thomas was enjoying his agreeable new life as the future heir to the Trewern Estate in Newpenwyn.

Cynthia had fallen pregnant on their wedding night and bore him a son just a week ago, and he was proudly enjoying the ceremonious smoking of pipes and clinking of sherry glasses with a select few of his local huntsmen celebrating the birth.

News had reached Thomas from his mother of the tragedy of the wretched girl Mary, but he didn't allow any further consideration of his part, preferring to believe she must have tripped and fallen into the canal instead. A verdict of *'suicide while temporarily insane'* had been passed by a jury in the Bridge Inn some time afterwards, and rumours were she had succumbed to something that had turned her insane while foraging. So how was either scenario his fault? As for hurting her feelings, he abided by the written words of John Lyly's novel, *Euphues: The Anatomy of Wit*, and his favourite quote.

"The rules of fair play do not apply in love and war."

He used this saying often, it never failed to raise an agreeable response from his male counterparts.

Currently, the gathering of six lounged in the games room and were enjoying a card game of *Don* when they heard the scream.

A flustered housemaid rushed into the room and addressed the shocked faces with an alarming announcement.

"Sir, I'm terribly sorry to interrupt, but there has just been a most frightful incidence, Madam Cynthia has urged me to fetch you at once!"

Upon entering the nursery moments later in a burst of commotion with staff members following him, Thomas stopped dead in his tracks at the pitiful sight in front of him.

Standing there by the crib, her body shaking with violent sobs was Cynthia, clutching their dead child to her breast.

Thomas turned to the enormous sash window and walked towards it speechless. His hands flew up to his face as he looked down towards the gardens and lake below in utter disbelief and shock. The blue drapes framing the window reflected in the glass and as the flurry of activity began to fill his world behind where he stood, his eyes quickly fixated on the figure standing below.

Grey and transparent, the ghostly figure of Mary stood there dripping wet. Her arms hanging by her sides, her dress cloth clinging to her swollen stomach her lifeless black eyes stared through his, and his stomach lurched with nausea as he felt the power of her vengeance and destruction plunged deep into his soul.

THE BUTCHERS SECRET

Monmouthshire Merlin, 1875.
ABERMYNYDD. SHOCKING CASE OF SUICIDE.
On Tuesday night last, Mr. Bryn Jones, butcher, Cloth-street committed suicide by cutting his throat. He said Goodbye Charlotte to his daughter and went upstairs into the garret. Fearing something wrong they called in the assistance of Mr. Jones, landlord of The Rat-Catcher Inn, and upon going upstairs found the deceased in the garret in the act of cutting his throat. The wound was a most fearful description. Deceased fell forward on his face. He had been rather strange in his manners lately.

    Charlotte was just brushing her hair, she counted 100 strokes before placing the thinning brush face down on her wooden dresser. She took care to avoid scratching the shiny tin back which was prettily shaped like a shell. It was one of the very few treasures she had.

"CHARLOTTE?" boomed the voice of her father from the bare floorboards beneath her.

"Coming Father!"

She knew this was not actually a request as such, she knew it meant hurry up and get to work. Charlotte took one last glance in the mirror and sighed. She was an attractive girl, albeit rather plain looking but her skin was porcelain white which highlighted her chocolate brown eyes and her hearts shaped face was framed by a heavy curtain of waist length shiny chestnut hair in which she took great pride.

She fixed it back into a tight bun and begrudgingly descended the stairs to the small butcher's shop below and taking her position behind the counter, fastening onto her skirts a white pinafore.

Bryn Jones, Charlotte's father, was in the room at the back of the shop, halfway through butchering a pig. His face was blank as his sharp knife worked its way expertly around the flesh, removing body parts with a silent skill that would rival a surgeon in their precision.

"Five rabbits all shot at dawn this morn, still warm for you miss!"

A cheerful voice belonging to a local man captured Charlotte's attention as he swung the furry bodies onto the counter with an ungraceful thud. Charlotte could not help but let out an ear-splitting scream, such was the fright.

Bryn Jones did not falter when he heard the piercing scream.

"Get that vermin off my counter Evan Gardner or so help me God I will skin you alive if you frighten me like that again!" she shrieked.

Amused, and with a twinkle in his blue eyes, he grabbed the paw of one of the animals and waved it at Charlotte.

"Hey, put me in the pot and make me into stew!" he mocked in a high-pitched tone.

Charlotte tried to hide her amusement but failed to conceal the smirk on her lips before she turned her back to Evan.

"Put them out the back with Pa, he will see to them but don't be expecting much, rabbits tough this time of year, the grass is not sweet."

Evan swung into action and strolled into the back room, as Charlotte straightened up to greet the first customer of the day.

Out in the back room, Bryn Jones was standing back wiping the blade of his knife with a cloth and admiring his handiwork when Evan strolled in.

"Morning Mr Jones I have killed for you sir," he said.

Bryn Jones's eyes flitted over the rabbits before allowing his head to nod in acceptance, he indicated with a second nod for Evan to place them on the stone block in the corner of the room.

Evan was 19-years-old, and quite a skillful hunter. He had been providing game for the Jones Butchers for three years. Often, he would be up at 3 am, stalking the woods on the outskirts of AberMynydd before walking three miles on foot to bring his wares to town.

Bryn Jones had been kind to him, often giving him fresh goods such as eggs and butter which were gratefully received by Evan, for his widowed mother was reliant on him as the eldest of seven siblings, to provide. He repaid the goodwill by giving him first refusal on the wares.

But Bryn Jones was not himself today. His usual cheery response had been missing lately, and as was becoming the norm, he did not look up, he merely placed the knife that was in his hands down on the surface and without comment left the room. He walked past Charlotte who was wrapping up half a pound of bacon for Mrs. Withers.

"Good morning Mr Jones, how are you?"

He appeared not to hear, and he walked right out of the shop.

"Well I never did!" sniffed Mrs. Withers, who feigned insulted very well.

Charlotte simply smiled apologetically at her and shrugged. Charlotte, she had noticed her father had not been himself recently. She presumed it was because he had been drinking excessively since the horrific murder of her mother Martha a year earlier.

Now, Charlotte and her father were alone in the shop, her older three sisters were all married and living with families out of town. With Charlotte's guidance in her father's monetary affairs, they managed very well on the butcher's income. The meat was always in demand. Living in the centre of the market town, and despite there being four other butchers' shops in Cloth street, the slaughterhouse kept them all well supplied, and people came from out of town to buy from them.

"Ay somethings not right with your Pa, so it's not," muttered Evan, who was standing in the doorway. "None of my business, but anything I can do to help like?"

Charlotte frowned, being a private person, she was unsure of how to react to the question.

"No? No of course not, but...thank you, Evan," she replied.

She turned to look out the window at her father as he walked in the opposite direction of the shop, his head was hung low, and suddenly Charlotte noted he seemed smaller somehow than he should be.

She had noticed he'd been disappearing a lot lately. Going for walks alone late at night, coming back smelling strongly of drink. She knew there was something amiss, but hoped that he would get through his grieving in his own time.

Johns own footsteps resounded around inside his head, one two, one two...but he was aware there was a second footfall. As Bryn moved his body rhythmically unfaltering in his gait, he made his way down Castle walk and to the meadows below.

Alone, at last, he heard the voice speak to him once more.

"It's time!"

The voice spoke with a strange accent, raspy, and whispering deep in his ear.

"ARRGGHH!"

Falling to his knees, clutching his head, Bryn would have been a pitiful sight had anybody been witness, for underneath the great oak tree was a broken man. A man destroyed by the voice that followed him tormented him…forced him to do such terrible things.

"You enjoyed it!"

It mocked and sneered, yet Bryn knew it was true.

He *did* enjoy it.

The adrenaline he felt rushing through his veins that night was unrivalled. The power he had over his victim, at the moment of surrender, made him feel like he was King of the world. At that final moment, moonlight hit the blade, and it flashed a glint of light on the knife causing him to pause momentarily. He saw the reflection of the horrific face behind him, twisted and contorted with a wide-eyed grin the demon urged him on as he sliced the pathetic woman's throat from ear to ear…he felt euphoric.

Mary Withers body was found the next day.

She was slumped in a puddle of sticky black congealed blood, it had been the talk of AberMynydd. The feeling of satisfaction Bryn had felt had lasted only a few hours, however, and profound anxiety soon started to sink in.

The voice stopped for a few weeks after that, deserted him, it had permitted him to fret about being found out. Sent to face the hangman's noose alone.

He had increased his visits to church and prayed more dutifully than ever, but the anxiety deep down was still there. He felt sullied and muddled. He knew that Mary Withers was a woman with loose morals, selling herself on the streets to keep her brood of brats alive who were nothing but thieving scallywags themselves. The town needed cleaning up. Women disgusted him more and more, they were all the same – except for his precious Charlotte. But he couldn't shake the feeling the task itself shouldn't perhaps be so pleasurable.

"She has to go!" hissed the voice louder this time. "She is going to be just like her mother, she needs to die before she spoils! Do it! Save her!"

Black shadows swirled before his eyes, he couldn't focus. He lay back on the grass the cold, damp, autumn leaves which were decaying underneath him, and he could feel they were crawling with bugs. He began to imagine them infesting his brain eating away the parts that made him do such horrific things.

How could he continue?

Charlotte was indeed getting too much, he looked at her face and saw her mother. He swore she knew. Her mother's soul was morphing into her, telling her what he had done, he knew she would soon find out, and that would not do at all. He loved Charlotte, she was all he had, and yet Bryn knew her fate would be the same once the curse of her beauty mislead her into using her feminine qualities to her advantage, as they all did, eventually.

He had wondered about telling her. How her mother had been carrying on with the landlord of the Kings Arms. How he had seen them together that night, meeting in a dark alleyway off Nevil Street, a clandestine meeting that had resulted in a bloodbath once he got her alone. Her eyes had pleaded with him as he had slit her throat, but his hear had been ripped from his chest that day. Unable to forgive her, she was no better than the others. How could he risk Charlotte finding out what type of woman her dear mother really was?

The truth would ruin her, poison her purity, and turn her into another that needed eliminating.

There was only one solution. Bryn had been thinking about this for some time.

Several hours later, Charlotte was just turning the metal sign over on the shop door to read, closed, as her father pushed the door open, startling her. Outside it was growing dark, and the smell of booze assulted her senses as he entered the shop.

"Father? Where have you been? I need help to sort the pig out before it all goes to waste, you just left it there."

She spoke to his back as he walked past her and began to climb the stairs.

"Goodbye Charlotte," he said.

THE BRYNMARSH GHOST

Evening Express 19th April 1905
Dylan's Bed Rocks Violently.
The Brynmarsh ghost has been at work again and as before it is Dylan, Mr Pritchard's little boy, who is its victim. The child firmly believes that he has seen the ghost. His father is now obliged to sleep in the same room with him as the bed in which he sleeps is sometimes seen to rock violently.

Following the supposed instructions of the ghost, the floor of one of the attics has been removed and a cap has been found, stiff with something, though what the substance is it is impossible to tell at this distance of time. A few remains of human origin have also been found.

The necessary permission has not-yet obtained from the landlord to open the large chimney at the top of the house, which would necessitate the pulling down of part of the roof, but the tenant hopes to obtain this permit.

Dylan lay under the bedclothes that night sweating profusely. His breathing was fractured by the claustrophobic stale air which smelt of damp wool.

Yet he doesn't move a muscle. His eyes squeezed tighter, so hard that he began to see stars.

"Why is it that I close my eyes to shut out the world, and yet all it does is open up a new one?" he thought briefly.

He tried to lose himself in the dark world beyond the present. Explore the deep abyss that his eyelids were offering him, an escape from the current situation he was in, but he couldn't.

11-Year-Old Dylan was small for his age with an unusual appearance. He had an unsightly hair lip that caused a speech impediment, although the stares this attracted from strangers hindered his speech more. His shock of red curls distracted from the disfigurement somewhat, and his eyes were the palest blue giving him the type of appearance that many found unsettling. He had learned quickly that to stay silent and out of sight was favourable to both him and his family. He spent most of his time in the second-floor back bedroom that housed a bed, small bookcase, an oil lamp, and an ottoman chest. His few cherished belongings were his books, and he prized the escape they gave him from the world, reading such gems as *Treasure Island* over and over, so much so that the pages wore thin.

Tywyll House was an imposing three-story structure with many rooms. It had previously been an inn and a Bank. Today his stepfather, Mr Pritchard, conducted his business as a solicitor and Court Clerk in the offices on the ground floor.

Dylan's stepmother was busy helping with the family business affording her children little time, but there was staff that kept him well fed and warm. Still, he spent many hours alone in his room preferring his own company as his own adopted siblings did not want to include him in their activities, saying he was, 'weird.'

Dylan had always known he was adopted. Since being small, he was acutely aware of the fact and had always felt displaced somehow. Despite the kindness of the Pritchards, he had never felt like he *really* belonged anywhere or that he was wanted by anybody.

His real mother and father had both been killed. His Father had been murdered, shot by a dangerous man, and his mother died in a horse and carriage accident when he was a baby. There were no photographs or pictures, and he always wondered what they looked like. Of course, he was very grateful for the Pritchard's taking him in and was often reminded how good they were to give him a home and an education.

His mother had been Mr Pritchard's sister. He spoke kindly about her sometimes which was a tremendous comfort, though Dylan kept his emotions inside. Mr Pritchard did not like to see boys cry, it was considered a sign of weakness.

Dylan's bedroom was situated at the bottom of a long corridor, somewhat away from the rest of the house, and reached via a small flight of four stairs. Outside his door was a further flight of seven steps to a permanently locked garret room above. It suited him, and he had always preferred the quiet part of the house.

Until recently.

His awareness could not shift from the footsteps walking towards him slowly in the dark. The creaking floorboards confirming that she was still there. He had seen her as he woke suddenly about ten minutes earlier. Upon opening his eyes, he had sensed her icy cold presence and there she was in the corner of the room staring at him. The woman was an alarming figure robed in a black Victorian dress with dark rings under her eyes and pale grey skin.

He had stolen only a fleeting glance at her before he had reacted. Hiding under the blankets, he sensed that she was urgently trying to tell him something, but he didn't want to find out what it was.

He was petrified...

At times like this Dylan found that it was best to hum a tune, it helped to block his senses so he could no longer hear the footsteps approaching. He began to hum random notes *la la la numnah nee.*

Suddenly the covers were yanked back abruptly, and Dylan screamed out in horror.

"NO!"

"Dylan! What's all this commotion about my lovely? Why were you out of your bed again? It's nearly two o'clock in the morning!"

Whispered the soft female voice of Ellie the housemaid, who was standing in her white nightgown holding up a lamp, and shaking Dylan with one hand.

Ellie was a nineteen-year-old girl from the South Wales Valleys. She looked fragile and pale with red hair and freckles splattering her nose, Dylan liked her, and she had taken to him, often they exchanged warm smiles. She was probably the only person that had never seemed to notice his infliction. If she had, she hid it well choosing instead to see his soul, taking the time to understand his quirks and various nuances. They had struck up a good friendship in the three years that she had been employed by his family.

Looking up at her relieved Dylan burst into tears. Leaping forward he grasped on to Ellie's arms and sobbed, "She was, here again, Miss Ellie! The woman...I saw her, she was stood over there! In that corner!"

Ellie's eyes widened, and she turned holding her lamp up to the corner of the room where Dylan was pointing. The shadows danced, and cobwebs flickered tauntingly in the candlelight. She lowered herself to sit on the bed.

"Did she speak to you this time?" she whispered, the fear in her voice tangible.

Dylan shook his head slowly.

"You must try to communicate again the way I told you to? Spirits usually have something to say, there is nothing to be afraid of."

Reluctantly Dylan nodded and straightened himself up on the bed.

Ellie spoke quietly.

"Do you wish to speak to us spirit?" she said. "If so, tap once for yes and twice for no." There was a silence as the pair breathed slowly and measuredly

The first tap came.

The sound came from inside the chimney breast, a single loud knock that made them gasp and swallow, their shock like a lump of meaty gristle.

Ellie spoke again.

"Are you trying to show us something?" she continued.

Another loud thud came from the chimney breast to which they both leapt up startled and ran to the doorway, only to bump straight into Mr Pritchard who upon hearing a series of footsteps and bangs had roused from his bed and followed the noises to investigate.

"WHAT is the meaning of this?!" he bellowed. "You girl, I shall speak to you in the morning! Leave at ONCE!"

Poor Ellie scurried past him, her head hung low.

"Yes, Sir, sorry Sir," she muttered, blood rushing to her face.

Dylan opened and closed his mouth several times before the words could come out.

"I ... I umm ... g... gho.. st."

He stuttered awkwardly, trembling now with a fear entirely different to the one he had felt five minutes previous.

"Ghost?" remarked Pritchard, before chortling and exploding into a guffaw so loud that his ruddy cheeks quivered and his fat belly shook under his housecoat.

Pritchard was a tall man, over 6 feet with a receding hairline and a pointed nose. His eyes rarely met with those of his 'son', choosing instead to bury in piles of paperwork rather than acknowledge that his youngest might appreciate his time. At first, he seemed genuinely amused.

"Well, I've never heard anything so–"

The knocking sound from the floor above started lightly at first and cut through the laughter like a rumble of thunder marking the imminent promise of a storm about to come.

Dylan backed into his step-father for comfort, an unfamiliar move as was the reaction of Mr Pritchard to place one hand on his shoulder. The tapping sounds grew louder in intensity, this time accompanied by scratching and scraping like someone had rusty nails dragging across a blackboard.

"WHAT IN THE DEVIL?!" shouted Pritchard, looking at him in disbelief then he pushed his youngest harshly back into the room. After snatching up the oil lamp and backing out, he slammed the door shut and threw across the bolt.

"I'll teach you to play tricks on me boy!" he bellowed. " I've no time for this, now get some sleep, we will talk tomorrow!"

"N... N... NO! W... WAIT! FATHER!" cried Dylan getting up and lunging at the wooden door desperately grasping the door latch and pulling with all his might to open it but his pathetic physique failing him. Sobbing and defeated as he heard his father's massive footsteps fading away down the corridor he slid down, still facing the door.

The sounds stopped as abruptly as they had begun.

As Dylan knelt by the door his forehead against the frame, he felt an icy cold blast of air behind him, and he knew. Her presence was back, and as his breathing slowed his heartbeat picked up the pace. Once more he closed his eyes and slipped into the dark world behind his eyelids begging the explosions of light to take him away to another place far far away.

The morning light woke him, streaming through the small window above his bed. He had no idea how he had fallen asleep, but he had slept on his knees by the bedroom door, his tiny body stiff and frozen. Slowly taking in his surroundings, he noticed something lying on the floor about three feet away from him.

It was a key.

After breakfast, Dylan had lessons with the private tutor who came to the house. Sat in the schoolroom with his siblings he stared out of the window twiddling his pencil, yawning sleepily, and trying to ignore the sniggers of his older brother William.

"Wooo, Dylan! The ghost is going to kill you tonight!" he mocked.

His bovine nose twitched habitually, shrugging his wire spectacles up and down which in turn made his magnified eyes bounce.

"William! Silence! Read your poetry!" snapped Agnes Jenkins, the plain looking 30-year-old tutor, her hair drawn back into a severe bun doing no favours to her featureless solemn appearance.

"Dylan, you may be excused. I hear you had a bad night, so I suggest you go and get an afternoon nap before dinner tonight. Your father has invited guests, and we can't have you falling asleep in the soup!"

Kindly smiling she picked up the book from Dylan's desk and placed it under her arm before pointing at the door permitting him to leave.

Dylan smiled weakly and stood up, scraping his chair on the floorboards as he made his way out of the room knowing full well that his family wouldn't be inviting him to join them for dinner. If they had guests, he would be getting the customary tray in his room. He had heard his mother remark once that his face put people off their food. Dylan walked up the stairs from the schoolroom and wondered about Ellie. He desperately hoped she was not going to lose her job.

Trudging up the corridor, he stopped for a moment and looked at the wooden door at the end and sighed. He needed sleep but dreaded being alone in that room again, his only comfort was that it was still daylight for another three hours. He put his hand into his pocket pulling from it the key he had found earlier. The rusty iron article sat snug in the palm of his small hand.

He knew what it was for.

There was no doubt in his mind that it wouldn't work. Moments later he slipped it into the lock in the garret door housed above his bedroom and turned it slowly.

He felt the click of the lock unfasten.

With trepidation, the sleep-deprived and exhausted Dylan pressed down on the handle, pushed open the door, and entered the room. It had gotten to the point where he almost didn't care if the ghost was there waiting to slay him. He knew he would instead surrender to her, rather than lie in bed another night feeling her ominous presence in the room tormenting him with her scratching and tappings, yet even in his acceptance of all these things his heart started to pound so hard he could feel it pulsating in his throat.

The room was dark, no light source available. Dylan propped the door wide open with a battered leather case nearby, allowing the weak light of day from the corridor to decant into the room. As his eyes adjusted, he gazed around at his unfamiliar surroundings. Colossal dust sheets covered irregular shapes around him. As far as he could remember, nobody ever came to this part of the house.

His instincts took his eyes to the chimney breast which he knew travelled downwards and underneath was his bed. This was where he had heard the tapping sounds.

Taking a deep breath, he walked over to the area, careful not to trip over the various anomalous objects in his path.

He paused hearing a sound behind him, he could have sworn it was an exhale of breath.

Nothing.

He continued.

At the chimney breast he put his hand out and started to feel the brickwork, it was rough and sharp in places, and he realised as he pulled his hand away covered with filth, soot, and cobwebs. He shuddered and reached out again only to simultaneously hear the door slam shut and find himself shrouded in blackness.

"I DON'T CARE!" he screamed terrified, his whole body began to shake. " WHO ARE YOU? WHAT DO YOU WANT FROM ME?!"

But with a twist of sense, his surprise at finding his speech bright and bold was more shocking than the revelation that he was trapped in the garret alone in the dark.

Dylan steadied his breathing. With his voice had come a wave of self-assurance he had never felt before. He spoke steadily and with clarity for the first time in his 11 years.

"Show me what you want lady, I am not going to be afraid of you."

He sat down on the spot where he stood and closed his eyes. The lights in his eyelids swirled around, and he concentrated hard on them, no longer wishing to be sucked away into another world, this time he focused on them allowing the picture to form. Like blobs of oil paint dripping onto the canvas the colours formed shapes, and slowly he began to make sense of them.

He saw the woman step forward with her arms outstretched, her dark eyes held his gaze then dropped to a box in her outstretched hands. Calmly Dylan spoke.

"Where is the box?"

And then at once, he knew. He opened his eyes and crawled across the floor feeling his way to the door which creaked open as he approached it. He hardly paused for a moment before running down the seven steps to his bedroom below, opening the door and running to grab his oil lamp and matches quickly lighting it.

He went back up the stairs to the garret. The glow illuminated the small room at once, and his eyes travelled to the chimneys breast. Moving aside a few wooden chests he scanned the brickwork until he saw it. A small symbol of a heart drawn in black was scraped onto a stone set about five inches from the bottom of the chimney. Bending down Dylan gently felt the stone, and sure enough, it moved smoothly. He eased it forward using his stubby nails and exposed a cavity behind the rock. Reaching in with his left hand he felt around and pulled out a small box the size of a book.

Trembling, he opened it.

Inside he found a bundle of handwritten letters and photographs tied with red ribbon along with a tiny box. He picked up the little box and pushed open the lid, to reveal where a beautiful rose cut emerald ring sat, its facets catching the oil lamp and making him gasp in wonder.

Hearing footsteps coming up the corridor, Dylan quickly shoved the contents back in the box and under his shirt, quietly grabbing his lamp he made his way back to his room just in time to lie on his bed and pretend to be asleep as Ellie walked in carrying a tray.

"Ellie!" cried Dylan, relieved to see her familiar face.

Ellie grinned back at him and entered the room as he sat up on the bed. Placing the wooden tray of steaming food on the ottoman, she turned to look at Dylan. Sensing the change in her friend and immediately noting the changed atmosphere in the room, its heaviness had lifted and the late evening sent a stream of sunlight into the room as she smiled back at him knowingly.

"You've spoken to her!"

ELLIE JENKINS STORY

"Ellie!"

The fragile female voice was barely audible from the back room.

"Yes Ma?" replied Ellie.

"Show Mrs Withers through when she calls won't you my love? She will be here at ten sharp for her reading."

"Yes, Ma," replied the young girl.

Ellie was fourteen years and two months. She was a dainty little thing with red hair and freckles that covered her pretty little nose like a dusting of cinders on the hearth, they looked almost as if they might blow off in a breeze. Her porcelain white skin was flawless making her deep green eyes shine like emeralds. She was a striking looking girl.

Today she had been working in her parent's small village store since around six am, sweeping the floors, tidying the counters, and washing the doorstep before the first customers of the day arrived. Her father, Tom Jenkins, had been busy out back for hours now baking the bread. The smell of fresh loaves filled the shop and seeped out into the thick foggy morning air which hung over the village of Brynteg, deep in the Welsh Valleys. It was a welcome scent, for it offered a refreshing alternative to the sulphuric odour spewing out from the ironworks a mile away.

Ellie's mother was Ruth Jenkins, a forty-year-old woman with dark curly-haired and greying streaks. Her dumpy four foot five form sat on a low wooden stool in the corner of a stone pantry amongst the sacks of flour and slabs of dripping. Her long dress swept the floor around her feet picking up dust, and her buxom figure fitted snugly within the confines of the dull, faded material it was forced into. In front of her was a wooden crate over which a cloth had been placed, on it was a pitcher of milk and a pack of cards.

Ruth was laying the cards out in a row when a chime sounded signalling the shop door opening. She heard low voices coming through the doorway. Even with her poor hearing, she could make out the sound of footsteps as her daughter ushered the elderly woman, whom she recognised as Mrs Withers, into the confined space.

"Good morning Mrs Jenkins, and how are we today? Any better?" enquired the pleasant Welsh-accented voice of the visitor.

"Ah well, mustn't grumble Mrs Withers! There are some far worse off than me. I wonder did you hear the news of poor Jonathan Parry? Shock'en it is!"

Mrs Withers held up her hands and waved animatedly.

"Oh, my! Yes, that poor, poor family! Blown into a thousand pieces by the blast furnace, so he was! They say only his cap was left of him, found it on the wall fifty yards away they did! He didn't stand a chance!"

The women exchanged further words of sympathy about the deceased worker before their voices settled to a murmur. Ellie left the room and went into the small kitchen at the back to gather the last of the bread from the cooling racks.

Tomos Jenkins stood just outside the open door allowing the heat of the clay oven to vent hot clouds of steam into the still foggy atmosphere. He took a deep breath as she walked in. Mr Jenkins looked older than his forty-five-years, his receding grey hair exposing deep leathery grooves on his forehead. His six-foot tall figure was stooped, his hands knarly reflecting the years of heavy toil having taken its toll.

He had worked in the mines from the age of six and suffered a terrible injury to his right leg following an accident when he just turned twelve when a roof collapsed crushing it. He inherited his father's shop at sixteen-years-old, a move that probably prolonged his life and for that he was incredibly grateful. His face was red from the hard work of baking bread. He inhaled deeply, and welcomed the cooling air into his lungs, despite the sharp pain and the wheezing and coughing it caused.

"Your mother has been talking to Mrs Pritchard's housekeeper at Tywyll House in Brynmarsh, Ellie," he said suddenly.

Ellie faltered and stopped in the doorway, her arms full with the basket of loaves, she turned to look at her father.

"Yes father?" she enquired, already suspecting what he was about to say.

"Aye. A position has come up as a housemaid, and as promised, the position is yours. You start on Monday. Good people the Pritchards," he nodded his approval.

Ellie felt the flutter of anxiety in her belly, and her eyes dropped to the loaves in her arms.

"Yes, father," she replied.

There was also a sense of exhilaration in her stomach. Her life so far had been contained within the village, and she had never before ventured out of it. Stories she had overheard in the store from the Housekeeper, Mrs Eda Price of Tywyll House, fascinated her and she felt she already knew the family which comprised of a solicitor, his wife, and their four children.

She knew to get such a position was an incredible privilege and that working for a family like theirs would provide her with a good life. She would get her own bed, half a day off a week to come home and visit her family and she would be well fed. Yes...this was to herald the beginning of a new life for Ellie.

About an hour later, Ellie was wrapping up slices of cheese in paper parcels to stack on the counter when her mother and Mrs Withers emerged from the back room.

"Well thank you very much, Ruth. I shall take heed of your warning..."

She overheard the old woman saying before she roared, "Oh young Ellie! News travels fast, I hear you are to start work at Tywyll House next week?"

"Yes, indeed I am," replied Ellie smiling politely.

Looking at the elderly widow, she noticed her eyes were bloodshot as if she had been crying. This was nothing unusual, for visitors to her mother often left dewy-eyed. Her mother was a clairvoyant, and the older residents of the village considered her to be gifted in the realm of fortune telling. Mrs Withers was a regular visitor and paid her in kind with eggs and milk from the small holding that she held, which they in turn sold in the shop.

"Well, you will be sure to work hard, they are good folk. Your Ma tells me of the deformed un' they have adopted," she tutted. Her voice dropped to a low hiss, "My guess is he is a changeling child, or else Queen Mab paid him a visit!"

Ellie paid little attention to the gossip. It was the way of the women in the tight-knit community, to discuss the business of others. It was a well-known fact, the Pritchard family had adopted the son of Mr Pritchards sister, she had been tragically killed in an accident involving her horse and carriage ten years ago. Widowed, and only in her early twenties, her son Dylan had been her only child at the time.

"If it had not been for the kindness of Mr Pritchard, that boy would be in the workhouse!" continued Mrs Withers, shrugging her breasts up with her folded lower arms, which held a basket. This was not news, but after an hour of talking, she was now facing a shortage of gossip. It was a story she liked to repeat often.

With nothing further to add, she bid her good days and left the shop, the chime ringing her departure and reminding Ellie that not another soul had been in yet that day.

"Mother? Please, may I be excused to go and pack my case?" she asked.

"Oh, that will take you all of ten minutes. What do you need to pack besides the good book and your two dresses?" her mother gently mocked and smiled warmly, pleased that her daughter was showing enthusiasm. "Go on up, I will help you later to sew new buttons on your Sunday frock, and we shall see about getting you measured up for your uniform tomorrow. Fancy! Our Ellie wearing a uniform!" Mrs Jenkins winked at her husband who had come into the room, wiping his hands on a cloth having just washed the baking utensils. He nodded back, a twinkle of pride in his eyes.

As she turned to skip up the stone staircase in the corner of the shop, the couple exchanged knowing glances with each other. Ellie was their only child, and they felt blessed to have had her. After many years of wishing for a family, Ruth had suddenly become pregnant. The fact that Tomos had been impotent for several years was never discussed between them. Nor did either of them ever acknowledge the remarks made about where Ellie's red hair came from. They loved her, and that was that.

Moments later, Ellie was on the second floor of the building above the tiny shop front, standing in the bedroom she shared with her parents. In the corner was a bedframe with several crochet woollen blankets laid out neatly over it. A wooden chest of drawers sat beside it, upon which stood a candlestick with a wax melted half candle inserted. Opposite on the other side of the room was another bedframe, smaller with more blankets. A tatty looking doll sat on the top, her eyes looking in opposite directions, and her brown human hair matted.

A heavy set wardrobe divided the two beds, and there was a small table on which lay a wooden comb with several broken teeth, and a large pot washbowl with a pitcher stood inside it. Kneeling down beside the lower bed, Ellie dragged out from under it a battered leather case. She threw it onto the bed.

Opening the case, she then went over to the wardrobe and pulled opened the doors. Taking out a grey dress which had a faded pattern of sprigs of flowers on the front, buttons from the waist to the high neck, and a modest frill around the collar. She smiled, it was her best dress. She folded it carefully into the case, then opened the drawer in the wooden chest, taking out a small leather bound bible. Ellie's grandmother had given her the book, and inside it was an inscription in carefully written handwriting. It read, '1863 Property of Helen Williams'. It was her only tangible link to the woman she was close to until a year ago when she had passed in this very room of old age. Ellie smiled and gently placed the book into the case beside her dress. She then picked up the doll.

"Well, it's just you and me now!" she said to the doll wistfully hugging her close to her chest. Wandering over to the small wooden framed window on the other side of the room Ellie leaned forward and opened the window. It creaked outwards into the fog, and she leaned on her elbows to gaze out onto the street below.

Outside was cold and bitter, and there was no breeze. The sounds of the ironworks bellowed and roared, and black soot poured from above the rooftops in the distance. The acrid smell had been trapped by the fog and made Ellie's eyes water a little, but she was used to it. Out on the street below, she could see children playing on the road with a stick and hoop, while a cat shot out from an alleyway followed by an angry woman chasing it with her broom, which made Ellie giggle.

A huddle of women gossiped outside the shop.

She closed the window and sighed. Sensing a presence behind her, she turned round to face the room once more. Sat on the bed beside her case was the familiar smiling face of her grandmother.

Unwavering Ellie smiled back. She spoke quietly.

"And yes, I will watch over the boy. As you asked grandmother."

Ellie had been able to communicate with spirit ever since she was a baby, just like the generations of women before her. Through dreams and clairaudience, she was able to hear the voices of spirits, and she would babble away to them in her crib.

Grandmother had taught her how to channel efficiently, so Ellie was not afraid. Now, although the knowledge of being able to communicate with the dead was an unusual thing to bestow, Ellie had been taught not to take it for granted nor to boast about it. She knew others found it unsettling. She had known for some time that the boy at Tywyll House was to be significant in some way because her grandmother had told her to be his guardian, and although she did not know yet why, she knew her journey was about to begin, and she was rightly excited.

Yes, she loved her home and her family, but she was ready for the new challenge. She was eager to meet new people and begin her life at Tywyll House.

FLORENCE

Florence Williams gently dressed the young child in a clean white cotton gown and laid him down in his crib. She smiled kindly at him and tears filled her blue eyes as she did so, dripping salty warm tears onto his dress.

A smart woman, twenty-three-years-old, she wore her long chestnut hair in a fashionable chignon. Her black silk dress had been tailored in Cardiff and fitted her petite frame elegantly. She had been officially in mourning for her husband Frank for ten months and she still desperately wished for him to be here to see his son.

Bank manager, Frank Williams, had been counting the money at the end of a working day in February accompanied by his secretary Maud when the gunman had entered the building through the enormous red door framed by two columns at Tywyll House.

Florence had been two floors up in the flat they lived in when she heard the shots ring out and the blood-curdling scream which had turned her blood cold.

Running down the stairs and bursting into the bank she had been greeted by the most horrifying sight. Her husband slumped over his desk, a hole in his pale-skinned red head spilling blood over the blotting paper and inkwells, dripping onto the tiled floor beneath and pooling around his feet. His eyes were open and staring, and poor Maud was hysterical hiding under the counter in front of him, her pastel green dress splattered with blood.

Within moments the police entered the building having just run down the streets blowing whistles at the perpetrator, a dirty scoundrel that had scarpered with a significant amount of cash in a sack, his pistol still in hand.

It was not the most sophisticated murder but it had the whole of Brynmarsh talking in shock.

Florence had fainted at the sight, and during the course of that month as events unfolded she had begun to feel more and more nauseous. It was her younger sister Frances who had suggested she might be with child. The added shock of this revelation was too much to bear.

By the end of March the Bank had closed, and Tywyll House was on the market to sell.

In the weeks that followed Florence was heartbroken. She refused to leave the house and ate very little, hardly enough to nourish her blossoming body and the life it now contained within. She would sit for hours reading the letters that she and Frank had exchanged before they married. Letters that were written in blue ink, sealed with red wax, and hand-delivered. Letters that contained dark secrets.

Frank had confided in her how he had fallen in love once before with a married woman much older than him, a customer at the bank. He had been hurt when she declared that she could not leave her husband after a romance that was intense and lasted only a few short weeks.

He had never seen the woman again.

The fact he trusted Florence enough to bear his soul, only made her love Frank more. It touched her, and she had genuinely felt his pain. These letters were treasured, tied with red ribbon, the symbol of what had been a real love story.

In them, they would discuss their deep love for one another, their plans for the future and their desire for a son or daughter who would complete their family one day. They included a few photographs. One of their wedding day, their faces glowing with happiness and unlike most Victorian photography, they threw the rule book away and smiled. The other photo was of Florence herself, Frank had arranged for her portrait to be taken on her birthday as a surprise while she sat on a picnic blanket by the banks of the River Usk one heady summers evening. She was wearing a white dress and held a parasol over her delicately. Frank had remarked that he had never in his life seen any girl look more beautiful than she did that day.

Frank had proposed to Florence on her 19th birthday with a beautiful rose gold and emerald cut ring, one that took her breath away with its beauty. She had thought at that blissful moment she could never feel any more love for a person than she did for him at that moment.

They had married in Brynmarsh church six months later and been keen to start a family immediately. Unfortunately, the weeks turned into months, and as no child was conceived she had almost given up hope that it would ever happen.

Florence had tortured herself with the ring and the letters after Frank's murder. One day she had taken them up to the Garret Room where she had a secret hiding place. A loose stone where she kept a few valuables concealed a hole within the chimney breast. She didn't feel that a bank was a safe place for her belongings anymore and felt that at least here, she wouldn't have to look at the painful items until she felt stronger.

Looking down at the small child in the crib before her now as she relived the ordeal in her mind she felt nothing but profound sorrow at the irony. The love she had for her husband was matched tenfold for the child lying in front of her, his disfigured little lip tacked under his tiny nose exposing toothless pink gums. It only magnified the feelings of protection she felt towards him. He had a shock of fox red hair on his head, reminding her of his father.

The world was a forbidding place, full of evil and despair and with every cell in her body, she wanted this child to know the love that both his parents had for him, despite his infliction. She knew that Frank would have felt the same for his son, he was one of the kindest and most decent men she had ever known.

The upset of the whole murder was what she blamed for the way her son had come into the world. His traumatic start in life had continued to trend, and his birth into this cruel world had been premature and painful.

The night she had gone into labour had been a stormy one and the pains had begun to grip her late in the evening. Sat by the fire she had doubled up in pain as her waters broke, her sister thankfully had the knowledge to get her to the bedroom and undressed before sending the shocked housemaid out to fetch the midwife who lived in the nearby cottages. By the time the flustered and overweight woman had bustled into the room an hour later, Dylan had been delivered onto the bed and Florence was unconscious with the pain.

Florence flinched as the first memory of meeting her son edged into her mind. Like a splinter of glass in her heart, it was difficult to recall the expression of sadness on her sisters face when she eventually woke from her unconsciousness.

At first, she assumed the infant must have died, such was the look of sorrow on Frances' face. She had gently sat down on the edge of the bed and explained that the child was weak and unlikely to survive.

"WHERE IS HE!? I WANT TO SEE MY BABY!" Florence had shrieked as the local Doctor, a Dr Moss, had rushed to her bedside discarding his top hat and doctors bag. She had pushed away the smelling salts being thrust under her nose and her attempts to clamber out of bed were hindered by the onlookers. She knew something else was very wrong.

Florence had been told very gently by the doctor and her sister, that her child was born deformed and that it was kindest to allow him to die. She had sobbed for hours and felt like her heart had been ripped from her chest until later that day she had weakly asked her sister to bring her the child.

Reluctantly Frances had agreed and gone to the nursery to fetch the wrinkled pink being from its crib where it lay naked and by an open window. The noise the child made sounded like a newborn lamb. She gently swaddled it in a blanket, and carried him to her sister.

Entering the room, Frances softly closed the door behind her and approached her sister, who had her back to her.

"Are you ready?" she whispered.

Florence nodded.

Numb with exhaustion and pain she felt that right at this second nothing could destroy her soul any further. Right at this moment, she wanted to die here holding her child and join her husband in heaven.

As she turned slowly, she braced herself to look at the hideous disfigurement that was her firstborn only to see the most beautiful blue eyes fringed with fair lashes looking back at her. She gasped as she took hold of the child and brought it to her chest, the little noises it was making stopped instantly, his face began to root at her breast.

She did what came naturally and began to unbutton her nightgown.

"No Florence! You cant feed him...the Dr said not to!"

Florence shot a look at her sister that would silence an exploding mine causing her to stagger back towards to the door and run to get assistance. By the time she came back with Dr Moss, the child had warmed and lost his blue-grey skin tone, now turning to a much healthier pink.

"Dr Moss," began Florence. "My son has a problem with his mouth, I see that. But he has fed from me, and he is breathing. How can you possibly say he will die?"

Her eyes flashed angrily as she awaited his answer, but the look on his face and that of her sisters told her all she needed to know. Her son was not sick at all, he was merely ugly in the eyes of society. His inflections, however, did not stop the surge of love she was feeling ooze out of every pore in her body right now, and for the first time in months she felt she had a reason to live.

Several weeks later and here she was standing over his crib looking down at little Dylan, and his little face was beaming back at his mother like a ray of light. His beauty was radiated from within him. He was a good baby, barely cried at all and she hardly ever left his side not even for a moment. Even going against all advice she kept his crib next to her bed and breathed in his beautiful aromatic baby scent at every waking moment she could.

The day ahead, however, was worrying her and she couldn't put it off any longer. Her brother Pritchard had made an offer on Tywyll House, and she had to travel into town to sign the paperwork. She had trusted her brother's wife to care for Dylan while she was gone, herself a mother of three.

The agreement was that they would move into Tywyll House and her brother would conduct his solicitor's affairs from the rooms below that were previously the bank. Florence and Dylan were going to stay for a few months until they both felt strong enough to make a new life elsewhere, but in the meantime, she was grateful for her brother's gratitude in allowing them to stay in their home.

The paperwork had been drawn up in the previous weeks. Part of Franks last will and testament left the entire estate to his wife, and so she had to sign to agree to the sale with witnesses at the local solicitors.

"I will be home soon Dylan, my sweet darling son," she whispered. "And we shall be at peace and happy forever I promise. We shall move to the countryside where you will prosper away from judging eyes and dishonest townsfolk. You will have the life your father and I planned for you my adorable son."

With a tender kiss planted on his forehead she left the room, and a beam of sunlight shone through the rain-soaked window giving the place a warm glow.

The stray dog on the lanes about two miles from Brynmarsh was injured and in pain. It limped in agony along the track, it hadn't eaten for days, and was scavenging the remains of a dead crow when the horse and carriage approached it. Shrinking back into the shrubbery it cowered, confused at the terrifying thunderous noise that was approaching it fast. The sound of the horse hooves and the wheels crashing along the rough track grew to monstrous proportions, and the terrified animals instincts were to fight for its life.

As it launched its attack from seemingly nowhere, the dog sunk its teeth into the back leg of the mare causing it to rear up in agony and bolt in a frenzied panic.

What followed was a blur of hooves, cartwheels, and breaking glass. The dreadful sound of scraping metal, snapping wood and a woman's screams mingled and morphed with that of the sound of the horse as it tried to drag the flipped and mangled carriage while the dog remained attached to its leg. Kicking and lashing out with its hooves the horse fought to be free of its attacker, the dog was suddenly launched into the air, and with a brief loud yelp fell dead landing in a heap on the side of the road. The horse twisted itself up and away from the broken carriage galloping off down the track dragging behind it one wooden piece and the leather reins.

∞

The carriage was discovered not an hour later by a passing tradesman, lying in silence with one wheel still slightly spinning in the wind. Its drivers arm was outstretched and the only visible part of him as the rest lay crushed underneath. He was dead.

Inside the carraige lay a single occupant, it was Florence. Her eyes open and unseeing, her mouth wide open having been killed mid-scream as her head struck the carriage. The site of impact oozing congealed black blood.

DEAD HAUNTED 2

BLOODY MARYS' REVENGE

17th September 1892
TERRIBLE TRAGEDY AT ABERWAYNE.
SUPPOSED MURDER OF A WOMAN.
THE HEAD NEARLY SEVERED FROM THE BODY, SPECIAL TELEGRAM TO THE EVENING EXPRESS.

"It is stated that a terrible murder was committed at AberWayne on Friday evening. Late at night the body of a woman, named Mary Connolly was found in a secluded spot near the London and North-Western Railway Station with her head nearly severed from her body. Considerable excitement was created by the sad discovery, and from what can be gathered, it appears that the woman was enticed to the spot between eight and nine o'clock, and the deed was committed about that time.

It appears that she had only left Usk prison that morning, and was a short time before the discovery of the crime seen in the company of a man. The police, who were quickly at the spot, have no clue as to who committed the deed, or whether there was any motive for the crime. The inquest on the body will be held this evening.

> Another account says last night a young woman named Marie Connolly, who had that day been discharged from Usk prison, was found dead on the new road leading from Brecon-road, Aberwayne, to Union Lane. Her throat was cut, and blood leading from a small shed in a neighbouring garden across a cabbage patch to the spot where the body was found, and shortly before death, the woman was seen in a man's company. Whether the case is murder or suicide is uncertain."

Rhys Davies stepped shamelessly forwards onto the wooden platform. His arms bound behind his back, his head held upright as the white hood was placed over his matted lice riddled brown hair. The itchy rope of the hangman's noose was secured around his grubby neck with a rough tug, his beard caught in it making his dark eyes water.

His stomach grumbled, and he thought of the measly breakfast offered to him that morning in his cold gray cell. Stale bread and tea. He had not touched it. Not because he was nervous because he wasn't. Because it was unpalatable. He wouldn't have offered that muck to a dog.

The countdown began to 8am, the Prosser brothers, public executioners for the Welsh Towns gaol looked at their pocket watches as they counted. Waiting for the large clock in the tower above them to begin to chime. Dressed smartly in suits and bowler hats their expressions were grim as they continued their routine task in a composed manner. They stood four feet away from the chaplain, who stood quietly reading a prayer.

"I am the resurrection and the life, saith the Lord, and he that believeth in Me though he were dead, yet shall he live; and whosoever liveth and believeth in Me shall never die. We brought nothing into this world, and it is certain we can carry nothing out. The Lord gave and the Lord hath taken away; blessed be the name of the Lord."

The words were clear and added to the solemnness of the grim situation. The wardens restlessly shifted from one foot to the other, they had seen this scene played out many times before.

One...Two...Three...Four...

The arm of the clock bouncing past each second as it passed Five...Six...Seven, it began to chime the sound resonating around them.

Rhys's eyes were wide open. He could make out vague shapes in front of him through the grubby cloth hood. It stank a putrid and stale odor. It had probably been on the heads of many a filthy criminal before today he noted.

It was a mild winter day; the daylight only just breaking through. A drizzle hung in the air, causing his ragged clothes to feel sticky on his dirty skin. His groin itched. He dug his bare toes into the wooden trapdoor they stood on, waiting for the moment that they would sense it drop open into the bricked dark hole beneath. He speculated with mild amusement about how long he would be aware of space below while he swung by his neck. He did not really care for his life anymore, being sober for the first time in years on this dull, miserable day, and his hands shook behind his back with the withdrawal.

He felt weary in his 37 years and ready to leave this godforsaken earth, sullied by the very existence of people he loathed. He despised his life, existing in it full of hatred for anyone that spoke to him and he carried the attachment of being bitterly angry at having been brought into the world in a backstreet alley, dumped in rags on the doorsteps of the workhouse.

He had never known love. His first memories were of hunger and loneliness where he lay for hours on end in his own filth. He learned not to bother crying by six months of age because nobody ever responded. Beaten and abused and set to work as a pickpocket at the age of 5, Rhys had never known what it felt like to be happy. Opportunities came his way, but he had been far too absorbed in his own world of negativity and anger to recognize them as such.

Once, when he was just 8-years-old, a kindly old woman once took pity on the dirty scoundrel she witnessed stealing an apple from a cart in the street. Through his mop of black curls and his dark eyes, she had seen the potential, and she followed him down the alleyway to try and coax him to her humble home where a fire and some hot broth would have been waiting. But as she approached Rhys, he lashed out at her viciously, kicking out and squirming from her grasp before running away.

Another time aged 17, he attracted the attention of a young girl who lived on the same street as he did. She thought his brooding dark looks were attractive, but he never looked up from the ground to catch her gazes.

He could only ever gain a minute amount of pleasure from the temporary stupor that alcohol offered him. He was grateful death was about to provide him with a permanent solution to his misery.

"PULL!"

As the clock struck eight, the orders were issued. Dan Prosser pulled the lever, the trapdoors opened with a heavy clatter, and the rope went taut.

Davies knew his neck hadn't snapped. It gave him no desire to struggle, however, and he hung for several drawn-out moments waiting for death to take him into oblivion. He couldn't breathe, and the air compressed in his lungs squeezed his chest until it felt like they were on fire. He sensed his bowels release in a concluding flash of defiance and everything went black.

The first thing that he noticed after that was the noise.

He thought it was his own choking that was resounding inside his head, but it wasn't. Gurgling accompanied by a sickeningly familiar high-pitched wail permeated his brain. He blinked a few times, his awareness confused. . .and then he saw her.

She was stood in front of him about 2 feet away.

It was Mary.

Her head was hanging on her shoulder, severed almost wholly, it lolled sideways and quivered. Her eyes were staring right at him, black and dilated pupils, cold with death and the grin on her mouth was fixed, teeth-baring oozing black blood and froth her expression was manic and mocking.

The gurgling noise was coming from her. . .he noticed the blood bubbling out of the horrific gash across her throat and yet, he could not look away. Her mouth did not move but the wail was there, constant and on a loop, try as he might he could do nothing to un-hear or un-see the horror that was presenting itself to him. His eyes would not close, his body still hanging.

Around them, was a black abyss. Rhys attempted to speak, but no sound came out. His strangled neck sharply reminding him of the situation he was in. With sharp searing pain the creeping sensation of his skin beginning to itch before bubble all over with burning sores.

Mary. His mind flashed back to the reason he was hanged. That filthy immoral slut!

He murdered her in cold blood a few weeks earlier just like others before her, he slit her throat with a deep gratification.

The night he killed Mary, she had been drinking liquor all day in the places he liked to frequent. He already knew her well. Her trade in the pleasures of the flesh was well known, and he'd have no qualms about buying her services in the past. She had just come out of the Gaul after a 28-day stint for being drunken disorderly, and she was right back here, doing exactly what she knew best.

He sat and watched her knocking back drink after drink that afternoon. Lapping up the company of the men she was surrounded by, she was flirting outrageously and regaling them with her tales of the gaol birds. The tales of her antics were met with raucous outbursts of laughter every so often from her admirers, topped by her own screeching laugh. That laugh was vile, the sound of it made him wretch with revulsion. She sounded like a cat being strangled he thought.

Quite why Mary was so attractive to men Rhys couldn't figure out. Oh sure, she had all the womanly features one might expect for a two-pound romp in a hay barn, but her skin was ruddy, tanned brown and topped with a cheap rouge on her ruddy cheeks. Her hair was raven black and piled loosely on top of her head, sticking out from under a green felt bonnet which had seen better days and undoubtedly many nights with its back on a cold floor.

Davies spent that day watching her, his shifty eyes affording a glance over at her table every so often when she would catch him looking and smirk, her heavy-lidded eyes giving him a cheeky wink whenever she did so, hinting that she was still game for whatever he was.

Later that evening, warm and merry with the booze, she danced on the table to the delight of her gathering crowd. A fiddler busked in the corner of the pub while she flashed her bare ankles, kicking up her skirts and whipping her petticoats around with a drunken clumsy jig, falling from the height into the arms of the delighted men with a 'Whoops!' which was followed by more raucous laughter.

He watched her leaving the public-house through the course of the night, with one man and then another, returning after twenty minutes or so each time, a flush to her exposed chest. It was clear what she had been doing.

Sat with his beer, he spat on the floor with disgust, the phlegm in his throat another indication of the revulsion he had for the woman. He blamed her type for his existence on this pathetic plane, and for the disease and discomfort, he would now be forced to live out his days with.

Soon enough, Mary giddily sang her goodbyes to her audience having got all she could milk from the situation. She staggered as she left the building, still giggling as she bumped into the door frame clumsily and hiccupping before belching loudly.

He left it several moments before standing up, shaking out his cap and placing it on his head. He left his tin tankard still half full of ale. Slipping out into the foggy street unnoticed in time to catch a glimpse of Mary, the dark outline of her figure visible in the evening sunset before it disappeared around the corner onto Union Street.

The foul grimy odor that she emanated was eye-watering. He held his hand over her mouth to stop her from screaming and shoved her roughly into a cabbage patch. It was dark, but he swore he noticed a glimpse of recognition flash across her wide, terrified eyes, and she bit hard down on his hand drawing blood. He stifled an agonizing cry and lashed at her face slapping her hard and cutting her cheek open wide. He was now raging with fury.

Already manic with her for giving him a nasty disorder that caused him the chronic irritation and pain, the boils on his skin now infected had begun to spread. He was disgusted at himself for allowing her to contaminate him those months earlier. He knew he was doomed, the constant scratching and the agony he was in was driving him insane.

The fumes of alcohol mixed with the stench of rotten teeth putrid on her breath as he held her down. She began spitting in his face with defiance, and as she did so, fanned the flames of his fury even more. He ripped the pocket knife he had across her neck wrathfully, and she let out a guttural scream which merged into a spluttering, gurgling grim wail.

He stood up, his contorted face relaxing into a blank expression and he walked away leaving her slumped in the gutter bleeding to death.

Using the grass, a little way down the street, he wiped his hands of her blood before returning calmly to the public-house to finish his ale before walking home.

Several days later he walked into the police station and confessed to her murder. Tired of living, he hated the world. He was sick of going to bed every night and wishing he wouldn't wake up. Rather than commit suicide, he hoped that by confessing to his sin that he would be redeemed in the eyes of whatever God might or might not exist and go to a better place. Not that he was a religious man, but he imagined that there should be a better reality than the one he had now. The one Rhys Davies thought he deserved. He was better than this low life existence.

Now, though. . .he was looking at his nemesis. Was he staring evil in the face or was he the evil itself? He was suddenly not so sure.

The moans increased inside his brain. . .like a swarm of wasps, the groans and burbles intensified and he could do nothing to stop it. Mary's expression twitched and jerked and her black eyes not moving their focus from his. Now, from every corner of his vision, he was beginning to see more faces emerge, slowly looming up behind Mary.

First, he recognized the young blonde, a one-eyed prostitute he had strangled in his late teens . . . her bruised neck and swollen face were unmistakable. The last thing she uttered, *'God help me,'* through her choking, now added to the loop playing loudly in his head. There was Emma too, a simple girl with her pale freckly face and small green eyes. Emma was one of the girls who had worked at the local cotton factory, he had been irritated by her continual smiling and positivity so one day he caught her in an alleyway and stabbed her in the chest and stomach with a splintered shard of glass. . .the air rushed out of her lungs with a whistle, and now that's what he realized with utter horror was the continual sound he could hear.

Others appeared one by one. Every woman he had brutally taken from this mortal world was here now. They looked at him. Mocked him. And he was still hanging with his arms tied tightly behind his back. He knew he was dead. He knew. . .with a horrific realization that this was the other existence that he was due. How long it took him to come to this conclusion, he could not fathom because, in death, time has no concept. While we are alive, we know death will transpire, but when we are dead, all we have is infinity. To be dead is to face eternity.

Back at the gaol, a crowd had gathered outside the stone walls, and a roar of cheers and claps rose as the black flag raised and the death notice of Rhys Davies was nailed to the wooden doors.

His physical body was left to hang for an hour before being cut down, declared dead by the coroner and given a paupers burial in an unmarked grave within the prison walls. Nobody attended and not a tear shed that day.

Perpetuity of torture and pain prepared to wreak its havoc on the cold-hearted man, and now and forever more, he would know and experience what fear felt like. There was no escape from the horror he was in. Too late to start praying, for this being his fate. . .this being his Hell.

IN THE DEAD OF NIGHT

> "A peculiar report comes from Glanhafod, Castell Mill, where some people have been scared by the announcement that ghost has been seen in the graveyard.
>
> The hamlet is on the banks of Tenants Canal and the Haford river and lies about a mile west of Castell Mill. Amongst other "localities" is a cemetery, at the end of what is called Black Jack Fields, and the ghost has been seen making nocturnal peregrinations of this locality.
>
> The apparition moves about noiselessly and speaks to no one. Several people have been on special watch for 'her' (for it takes a feminine form). But, although they have entered the cemetery by the wicket that the ghost uses, they have not seen her, either in the pathways or amongst the tombs.
>
> Women of the neighbourhood are disturbed considerably by the rumours, but it appears (from our special respondent's report) that the young men going homewards from the taverns see most of the spirit."

Exhausted, Nesta Hughes wiped the brow of her firstborn for the hundredth time that night.

Afterward, she broke down and wept silent tears. The poor mite was delirious. Sweating profusely and with no energy to cry little Huw whimpered like a half-drowned kitten. His face was pale and ghastly gray, the dark circles under his brown eyes mirroring her own. His fair hair clung to his face making it appear darker than it was, as she tenderly pushed it back and stroked his forehead.

"Hush my sweet boy, Mammy is here, do not fret do you hear? Mammy is here."

She didn't think he heard her. Just three years into his life yet the signs were there that he was about to leave it. She knew because she had seen it before. Lived through the death of her own three sisters when she was six. She had escaped smallpox herself, but now, sitting here brought back the memories of how her own mother sat, just as she was now, nursing them.

To anyone else, Nesta might have been much older than her twenty-six years. Her salt and pepper long hair scraped back with string and not brushed in weeks. The skin on her face battered by the squalls of salty tears, and her once bright green eyes had stopped shining moons ago. Now, empty of hope, they only echoed the years of hardship and toil they had seen. The pain of this situation stung her heart like a thousand angry hornets.

A pile of dirty linen sat in the corner of the room, and it stank. Nesta didn't have the time to get it clean as this would mean leaving the bedside. The other women in the small row of houses had sympathetically brought her what they had spare. All refused to cross the threshold of the house for fear of the spread of disease.

The morning was breaking now, outside the cracked and dirty window. Nesta could see the orange sky slowly rising over the Black Mountains, casting rays of color over the low cloud aptly known as "dragons' breath" below. That cold January month had been bleak and dismal so far, the unforgiving winter months were dragging, and there seemed no let up. Mist and fog clung to the sooty brickwork that made the terrace of steelworkers' homes they lived in. An apt dank and dismal packaging for the human poverty that existed within them. Nobody dared to complain to the Ironmasters for this was at least a roof over their heads and protection from the elements. Something to be grateful for at least.

Earlier that morning John Hughes had left for his twelve-hour shift at the Glanhafod Steel Works. He had badly wanted to stay and support his wife but knew they could little afford to lose his job. They could scarcely find the money for food and fuel for the fire as it was. And it was an unforgiving winter. Without fuel, they had not been able to boil water to drink. John had seen many of his co-worker's children die in these past few weeks, and now, despite their despairing prayers, sickness and diarrhea had blighted the Hughes household. Little Huw, already cold and weak from lack of food had scarcely any stamina left to fight the aggressive disease that ripped through his system.

John knew that he had already lost the battle. He sensed that his last memory of his son would be that of him struggling for breath, writhing in pain on the bed. He could not afford a doctor and as he walked the dirt path to his home his eyes never lifted off the track once. Tired and worn from his shift, he had not slept in days, yet his bed was the last thing he wanted to see right now. It was the only one they had, and they shared it with little Huw. How he dreaded walking through the front door that morning.

Nesta heard the door below the small bedroom click shut and listened to the familiar sound of John taking his boots off. Usually, she would be eagerly waiting for her beloved husband to return home, a steaming pot of hot broth would welcome him before he would climb the stone steps to his bed. But this sad morning seemed to be another world, it was an ethereal moment which hung like the mist outside.

Just minutes ago, Huw had taken his last breath, with a gasp his little eyes had opened wide and looked into his mothers, desperate and silently pleading for her to help him, he had frozen. She saw his soul leave his broken little body as he became an empty shell. The most precious thing in her life had slipped from her grasp, and no matter how hard she had tried to hold onto him, extinct forever. Now, like torture, she had to watch as her husband would walk in and take in the scene before him knowing that he too would be shattered beyond all repair.

They sat for several hours on that bed that day, holding Huw and rocking him, singing his favorite songs to him. Nesta used all the last of the fuel they had to bathe him in warm water, cleaning his body from the soiling and the sweat. She had begged for the pain to stop hurting her child, but now she almost wished she could hear him cry out once more. For some miracle to save him and bring color back to his cheeks. Outside the window, they listened to children playing happily, delighted screams as they teased a cat. Angry words from mothers who very much needed a break from their children – Oh how the Hughes would like to be in their shoes right now.

There was only one knock at the door later that day. The local Minister Rev Harris, called. Word of the death, thanks to *"The Boy Jones"* had reached him. Nothing was secret where they lived. He solemnly gave his words of comfort and handed the Hughes written details of local paupers' funeral arrangements and left.

Methodists, John and Nesta, needed to protect Huws' innocent young soul from evil and the only way to do this was to bury him on consecrated grounds. But that would cost them money they did not possess. A pauper's burial would mean that Huw would be placed in a mass grave on a hill nearby with at least ten other dead children and the thought was nauseating.

Glanhafod chapel where he had been christened had a small churchyard but to bury him in this way cost almost a year's wages, and John had never been able to afford the £1 a week funeral policy. Despite going without food, himself some days he had used every spare penny to keep his child warm that winter. There was another option. He knew that the cholera epidemic had brought many funerals to the chapel in the recent weeks and the ground would be still soft.

He quietly told Nesta that they would have to wait until the dead of the night to carry their small precious son to the edge of the churchyard. To secretly bury him in a fresh grave. He would have to turn up for his shift as usual, but tonight he planned to slip away unseen under the cloak of darkness and get back to his stand shoveling coke into the blast furnace before he was missed. His co-worker Stan would cover for him if necessary, as he owed him a favor. Then he would meet Nesta, and together, they would carry their child to sleep until Christ revisited the earth, lay in the only place they felt would be safe and close to them.

Darkness arrived early in January. The evenings were long and unyielding. From five o clock every glimpse of winter sun would be covered, and tonight it was a clear sky, the waning moon casting its luminous shadows onto the world below. The deathly chill in the night air had dropped the temperature to well below freezing and ice was beginning to form on the top of the shared well where four women were attempting to break it with rocks. Nesta watched them from her upstairs window restlessly for a while before turning her gaze out into the night. Not wishing to turn around for the sight of her poor dead baby would still be there, laid motionless on the bed, wrapped in a white cloth.

John was heaping the coke into the furnace, it was crippling work. His bowed back hurt. His face black from grime, hid the blistering redness caused by the intense heat as the fire raged before him, melting the pig iron. He was barely four hours into his shift when the explosion happened. The blast echoed through the mountains like a sonic boom, shaking the very core of the valley. He was killed instantly along with five other men.

Quietly tiptoeing through the village, trying not to disturb the sleeping dogs that would alert their owners of an intruder, Nesta stopped still. When she heard the loud bang in the not too distant locality, she froze. There was no light, and she could hardly carry a candle as she was stealthily moving along in the shrubs clutching Huw closely to her chest. Occasionally stopping to crouch down she heard the raucous laughter of drunken dregs stumbling out of the Tavern and managed to stay out of the sight of a young couple giggling in the shadows of an alleyway.

She had no idea what she had just heard, but her mind was not thinking straight at that moment, and all she could think of was getting her child to the churchyard. John was late. She knew he would be trying to get away from his standing position at the blast furnace, and that time was not on their side. He could not risk the ironmaster noticing his absence or they would find themselves living on the streets before the week was out, aware that dawn would be upon them soon, so she had decided to go ahead and surely, she would meet him on the way.

The path that leads to the small wooden gate at the entrance to the yard was covered by an archway of ancient yew trees, their long sinewy branches like wizened arms shaking hands across the pathway, twisted and wise, reaching out to welcome those that entered the sacred ground. An owl hooted from above her, making her jump, and she nervously gripped Huw's body tightly to her torso.

Nesta sat for an hour under a large yew tree waiting for John to arrive. She could not shake the feeling that something dreadful had happened to him, but then again, not one of the thoughts that occupied her mind had been positive recently. It was intensely cold, and snow began to fall, soft icy flakes landed on her cheeks and eyelashes, but they did not melt.

She was shivering bitterly frozen. Sat there in the dead of night.

The numbness in her fingers mirrored that of her heart. As she sat there, she softly sang a lullaby so delicately it was barely audible.

"And if that horse and cart fall down,

You'll still be the sweetest little baby in town."

Rocking Huw tenderly, she gazed at the frozen little face in her arms. She so desperately wanted to feel warmth from her child and held him tightly, willing him to warm up and should God be willing to allow.

"PLEASE HUW! just open those eyes once more and look up!"

It would grant her every last wish she had.

When the first light of the new day began to crack through the night sky, she knew she had no choice. With all her strength she managed to stand upright and placing her little boy gently on the ground she used the dim blue, dusky natural light to locate the fresh grave that had been buried the previous day. Putting the flowers that had been left for the privileged, anonymous person beneath to one side, she began to dig.

At first slowly using her hands to move the earth, but then, besieged by a mother's determination she suddenly threw her entire body into the mission to shift the ground as much as she could, clawing at it with her fingers and nails, sobbing quietly as she worked. Two hours later she had made a hole that was enough to place Huw in.

Daylight was breaking through, and the birds were beginning to sing their dawn chorus as Nesta placed her son down, tenderly kissing his little forehead and taking a flower from the ones left for someone else onto his chest. She whispered *"goodbye my sweet boy. God bless you,"* covering his face with the cloth, she lowered her eyes and refused to watch him fade under the earth as she began the arduous task of covering his body again. As the last bits of earth were put back in place, the snow that had been coming down thickly began to layer a clean blanket of white as if helping her to cover him and her tracks. Before long Huw's resting place looked as undisturbed as the ancient graves surrounding him.

Filthy dirty, sore and broken Nesta dragged her body home to a cold, empty house. She was just able to break the ice on the well surface and fetch a wooden bucket of iced water to clean her filthy nails where the mud had wormed its way down through several layers of skin, making her weathered hands look like the shovels they had been used as. As she was approached by Mrs. Thomson, a neighbor from two doors down, she self-consciously hid her hands in her skirts and began to move away.

"WAIT! Nesta!" said the tired looking woman with her pinched eyes and toothless mouth. "Your John was on the furnace shift, wasn't he?"

Nesta stopped in her tracks and gradually turned to look at Mrs. Thomson. Nervously she nodded, not really wanting to hear the words that would come next as a slow realization began to dawn. She barely heard what was said next. The word *"blast"* and *"dead"* echoed around her skull along with the memory of last night's explosion coming back to haunt her.

The world began to swirl all around her. Blurred faces, stone walls and a bleak sky blended into a thick broth of nauseating vomit and Nesta felt her stomach twist as she wretched and wretched on the spot, dropping her bucket sending the iced water crashing to the ground. Her empty stomach squeezed and crushed her insides and unable to stand the pain she collapsed on the cobbles beneath her.

A small gathering of women had gathered at the scene and managed to lift Nesta's frail body to her bed, where her body succumbed to a churchyard cough in the hours that followed. Sick, shivering, feverish and unable to swallow any of the broth Mrs.

Thompson kindly offered, her destroyed soul had no will to live and she never really regained full consciousness, drifting in and out of a delirious fever.

The ghost of Nesta returned to the churchyard the night she passed away, unable to follow the light that came for her. Still badly wanting John to meet her there, she waits at the churchyard gate for John to come and say goodnight to Huw with her and occasionally when men are passing late at night, they see a glimpse of her pale white face in the shadows watching them.

DEAD HAUNTED COLLECTION

PRIVILEGED TO KILL

1862 Monmouthshire Merlin
FOUND DEAD.
Strange Discovery in Blackmoor.

On Monday a lad named Rowlands discovered the decomposed remains of a well-dressed man in Dragonhill Wood, Blackmoor.

A revolver was found beside the body, which was in a sitting posture, while the head was located a short distance away.

There was nothing on the deceased to lead to identification, but, from entries in a pocket-book, it is inferred that he was a commercial traveller.

The remains had been partly devoured by vermin, which probably accounts for the head being severed.

The last entry in the deceased's diary was dated April so that it is believed the man committed suicide about that time.

The boy who made the discovery says he had seen the body before, but, only from a distance, and mistook it for the stump of a tree.

Sir Ieuan Gethin arose feeling optimistic and eager, that bright, mild morning of September 1st, 1862. Hettie, the housekeeper, laid his tray of tea on the table in his bedroom and informed him that his hunting clothes were laid out in his dressing room. He nodded his thanks to her and sat up in his four-poster bed, pushing the luxurious white sheets back and stretching lazily.

He looked over to the doorway that leads into his dressing room, where he saw the china vanity bowl and a pitcher of steaming hot water ready for him to wash with. Hettie yanked back the heavy green velvet drapes using brass poles, allowing the waiting sunlight to erupt through the windows. The dull looking, nineteen-year-old girl daydreamed to herself. Imagining that it was like a golden stairway inviting her to climb it to the heavens, she paused for a moment to admire the swirling dust disturbed from the drapes dancing and swirling like glitter in the light.

Blinking and squinting for a moment as his sleepy eyes adjusted from the darkness like a butterfly emerging into the world from its cocoon, he set himself up in bed.

"Ah! What a beautiful morning!" he declared smugly, and with sudden energy, he swung his legs round to stand.

Hettie blushed as her Master stood before her, a handsome man of six feet four in his white cotton nightclothes. His dark, brooding eyes gazing out of the windows at the mountains and forests below the bay windows of his impressive manor house.

Unaware of how his masculine figure had affected the poor servant girl he strode over to the window to drink in the scene.

His long black hair was secured at the nape of his neck, and he sported a shadow of stubble on his face framing his square jawline. He swung round suddenly making poor Hettie jump backward, mortified that she was caught out admiring his broad shoulders.

Unaware and ignorant of any servant's ability to feel desirability, he threw an instruction to her.

"Have Wills prepare my rifle, I shall be shooting in the woods today. And have him arrange for my horse to be saddled, and I am taking two dogs too."

"Yes Sir," said Hettie, relieved to be dismissed as her face was turning a darker shade of red with every second that passed. She scuttled out of the room gratefully closing the door behind her.

Ieuan strolled over to the wash basin and poured the steaming water into the bowl before washing his hands and face. Rubbing his skin dry with the flannel he rubbed behind his ears and the back of his neck deciding against shaving.

What was the point?

Today he was going hunting he quite enjoyed the feral feeling occasionally it was a relief not to have to conform.

Patty, his wife, had gone ahead of him the previous day with the carriage to stay with his cousins at Windmarsh Manor, which stood twenty miles east of Blackmoor.

Uncle Terrance, the Duke of Breckshire, had passed away last month and had left the entire estate needing management, so they planned to stay for at least three weeks. Luggage had been sent ahead with his wife and vague instructions to expect him sometime the next day. Patty avoided him whenever she could and did not seek to spend leisure time with her husband. A marriage of convenience suited them both.

Today, however, was his first day off from business matters and he was looking forward to going out alone, doing the thing he loved the most.

Killing.

Half an hour later and Sir Ieuan was dressed in his best hunting attire. Brown breeches, dark tan leather boots, and a longline dark green hunting jacket finished with a handsome top hat.

His heels click-clacked through the great hall where large oil paintings of his ancestors hung. Their solemn pale faces watching him as he strode to the dining room where a breakfast of cold meat, fruit, bread, and eggs awaited him.

Two brown speckled pointer dogs welcomed him, excited to see their master wearing clothing that could only mean one thing. They were going out on an adventure, their happy tails wagged, and their pink tongues hung out as they padded impatiently up and down the room.

Finishing his feast, he placed his knife and fork down and sat back in his chair for a moment allowing his food to digest and he looked around proudly.

The dark wood paneled room was filled with hunting trophies.

All around him were the heads of creatures he had killed himself, foxes, bears, lions and tigers, huge stags with antlers, deer and hares, badgers and stoats.

Reminiscing about how he had made his first kill age just two years old, with the guiding hand of his father, the late Sir Alywyn Gethin.

They had shot a hare. With amusement, he recalled how he had screamed.

The sight of fresh blood had terrified him, as the loyal cocker spaniel had retrieved it, the limp furry body hanging out of the dog's soft mouth as it had brought the animal to the horrified child.

Still half alive it's back-leg twitching, and terrified eyes wide-open with blood seeping from the sockets, the sight had given him nightmares for weeks.

How his father had laughed at the childish reaction and how now, years later the memory had morphed into a happy one, and one that would mark his lifelong passion for field sports.

"We are privileged to kill, remember that boy and be proud!" his father had often said, and that statement filled him with self-importance.

Onlookers would watch him ride past with envy, as he rode his gray thoroughbred hunter Stanley through the village of Blackmoor accompanied by his faithful gun dogs.

He knew many men had risked their lives to poach on his land and damn he made sure nobody ever got away with it.

A public spectacle was made of anyone that dared to steal a kill on his property, he was merciless, and not even a pheasant was ever killed there without his knowledge.

Once he had caught a local boy of about 12-years-old in Greykeepers wood carrying a dead rabbit. He had dismounted and whipped the lad several times with his leather crop causing the boy to drop it and run whimpering like an injured dog.

Let that be a lesson to him and anyone else who saw the wounds on the boy's arms and back. *'They would think twice before poaching from HIS land,'* he had reasoned.

Ieuan was a handsome and prosperous yet unpopular gentleman.

His heart was cold. His narcissist ways exhibited rudeness and crass behavior all because he had wealth, power, and when he wanted, charm to make sure he got away with anything he wanted.

Marching boldly out of the house he left instructions with the staff he would not be back for dinner and not expect him until late. He mounted his horse shortly after breakfast at just after nine am and so he smiled to himself. He was now where he wanted to be.

Riding through his vast nine hundred acres of private woodland, his shotgun and revolver hung around his body in fine leather holsters. The silver stirrups cast dazzling rays of the early morning sunlight as they walked. Sir Ieuan ignored the peasants that tipped their hats good day as they passed, instead of looking through them, trivial small talk disinterested him, and he did not pass the time of day with ordinary folk.

After an hour or two, half a dozen pheasant had been dispatched, and boredom was setting in. He knew his woods were well stocked because he had ensured that by employing the best gamekeepers in Wales. The birds in these enclosed lands were surrounded by hedgerows and wild thickets and kept well within close range for shooting.

Where was the fun in that?

No, today his thirst for blood was intense, and he ventured much further out into wild and rural woodlands of Dragon Hill.

Dragon Hill woods were a place he often hunted foxes with the Blackmoor Hunt.

Galloping wildly through the trees, jumping hedgerows and streams, dodging branches and flying mud with the thunder of hooves and the shrill sound of the horn as they pursued their furry victim was his favorite past time.

He felt himself harden at the thought and he urged his horse into a gallop.

The power of the kill the thrill of the chase and the final surge of gratification and euphoria it gave him when the dogs finally fell onto the fox, ripping it from limb to limb. Hearing an animal screaming in agony simply heightened Ieuan's exhilaration. His pulse was racing now, and he galloped on, his dogs chasing beside him yelping with excitement until they reached a clearing, far away, deep in the woods now, several miles from his home.

Dismounting, and tethering his horse to a fallen tree he reached out to release his guns from their holders. Taking a rest on a thick fallen oak to slow his breathing down he took in his surroundings. He did not recognize this part of the woods and felt a little disorientated. The dogs were sniffing around, exploring, tails in the air and noses to the ground, sniffing for any potential prey.

But today Sir Ieuan was not interested in any old critter.

Oh no.

Today he was after the biggest and the best, and he wanted to experience a high like no other.

He desired to take the most powerful creature he could and prove what a powerful man he was to all who knew him.

Picturing the look of awe on the faces of his cronies when they would lay eyes on The Beast of Dragon Hill, mounted on solid oak, inflated his already huge ego. He had for some time now, imagined the stuffed stags head, in pride of place above the brand new twenty-foot square oil painting of himself that he had commissioned with a local artist.

Depicted standing proudly with his foot on a tree stump, with his dogs and Stanley the horse stood beside him, his gun on his shoulder, the rolling hills were to be in the backdrop. He was to unveil the painting next month at the annual Hunt Ball, which he hosted at Blackmoor Manor every year.

It would be a pinnacle moment for him to see the looks of envy and admiration on their faces when they saw he also had the ultimate trophy of The Beast's head.

Several weeks ago, talk of The Beast had spread among folk at élite hunt meetings, and its existence had reached the sharp ears of Sir Ieuan . The giant red stag was rumored to be at least three hundred pounds of flesh standing nine feet tall and had apparently gained in its physique over the last two years.

As aristocracy, he was one of the few legally privileged to be allowed by law to hunt such a creature.

It was an unspoken rule that such animals be prized and allowed to live out the prime of its life, to rut and to breed with females until it had a good ten years of healthy bloodlines established.

The Beast must be, at the guess of the Hunting set, about ten years old now. The price of this magnificent head was high. Upper-class game enthusiasts were getting tetchy in anticipation of who might get to mount those enormous antlers on a plate, and several gentries came to mind, of whom would pay for the prestige of the kill.

But today he was resolute that the prize would be his.

The bright morning had by now turned to early afternoon, and the Indian summer had begun.

As he unwrapped the parcel of cheese and bread he had in his saddlebag and took a swig of whiskey from his hip flask, something caught his eye on the ground. He bent down and picked up the small leather-bound pocketbook partially concealed by the fresh falling early Autumn leaves on the ground.

Taking a bite from his chunk of sourdough he chewed leisurely, turning the pages out of mild curiosity. There was little in the diary after April, it appeared the owner was a traveling salesperson named William Thatcher, and it seemed like some sort of trade directory. He put the book into his inside pocket and pondered if the diary owner might be sleeping rough nearby.

The air was still, not a breeze to be felt. Stanley who had been nodding his head and blowing down his nostrils had stopped, his noble head held high, ears sharp, the horse stared over toward the thickets of foliage beyond the clearing where they stood.

The pointers also stopped and were looking in the same direction, bodies frozen still.

One front leg up and tails pointing straight behind them, noses twitching.

A branch snap sounded in the direction of the undergrowth, and the dogs uncharacteristically turned around and began to whimper. Fearing a poacher, he quietly placed his lunch down on the trunk of the tree and with sweaty palms picked up his revolver.

It was unusual for the dogs to react like this usually they were reliable as a front-line defense, they were trained to bark and alert their master. Sir Ieuan narrowed his eyes and frowned as he stalked whatever the animals had sensed. The dogs refused to follow despite his hissed demands, so he gave up and continued forward, disappearing into the dark wood.

Feeling his heart pound, he speculated that it could be anything as his body heat rose.

It felt like only moments but, several hours passed as Sir Ieuan paced around, crouching behind shrubs, hearing snaps and rustles but achieving nothing.

He felt sure that he was being watched by something but couldn't quite put his finger on by who or what. In all his years of hunting, nothing had ever led him a merry dance like this before. Human or Beast.

He just then noticed how the light was failing and that night was approaching fast. As dusk fell on the woods, it occurred to him he would be soon missed at the manor as he would not be returning within daylight hours now. He also realized that he had no means of light with him. As he looked up at the red sky, dark clouds were closing in, he saw the beginning of a Blood Moon rising beyond the incredible Welsh mountains.

He dropped his shoulders and just as he was about to consider defeat, he heard a branch snap behind him. His body stiffened, and for some bizarre reason, he found he could not turn around. Could not or would not, he wasn't sure. He stood there for what seemed like a long time, frozen to the spot, his heart pounding in his chest so hard he could feel it in his throat.

Every hair on the back of his neck stood on end as he urged himself to turn around steadily. He knew this thing was behind him, he could sense it. Bloody Hell, he even could feel it's breath...

The woods went deathly quiet around Ieuan. He shuddered as the eerie feeling crept over him like a thin veil, and his skin had a sensation like cobwebs brushing against it. Not a bird could be heard. Usually the woodlands would be alive with the early evening activity of wildlife, yet oddly nothing stirred.

Trying to stop himself from trembling with the uncertainty of what he was experiencing Sir Ieuan summoned all his strength and forced himself to turn on the spot to face whatever, or whoever was there. He turned his head and upper body first, keeping his eyes on the ground, and let out a startled gasp as he saw the vast cloven hooves just two feet away from his leather boots.

His eyes traveled slowly upwards until he found himself standing looking up and directly into the penetrating black eyes of The Beast.

Ieuan's mouth opened and closed several times, but no sound came out.

This creature was magnificent, beyond all belief.

Why this animal must be over twelve feet tall and weigh at least eight hundred pounds. Its incredible velvety antlers impressed a mighty crown on its head, and it stood within touching distance of him now. It's energy so powerful that Ieuan dare not even breathe.

This was something unbelievable and frankly out of this world. He took a steady step backward, but the stag made a sustained and measured step toward him, its eyes not faltering from its intense stare for a moment. With trembling hands, the shocked man gulped.

A large lump had expanded in his dry throat, and he could not swallow it down, and he barely knew of the hot wet dribble running down his legs.

He felt an unfamiliar feeling of horror. This was not like anything he had ever experienced in all his years of hunting. He had no idea that such a creature could exist and as his mind raced he tried to grasp his senses and steady his shock. He must not lose it now!

Slowly, very slowly, without taking his eyes off the stag, he curled his fingers tightly around the revolver he still held in his sweaty hand and released the safety catch with a neat flick of his thumb. He spoke slowly and lightly as he gradually raised his right arm up to shoulder level.

"There's a good chap! Stay right where you are my beauty!" he whispered quietly, his voice breaking, and gaining his composure. An angry sneer crept up onto his face. He was Sir Ieuan Gethin, and nothing would get the better of him.

The stag was motionless.

Ieuan shut one eye and focused on the end of the barrel of the gun. Determined to savor this moment for every drop of notoriety it was about to bring him.

Just before he pulled the trigger, a tremendous noise ripped through the sky. The great Beast raised its head and thundered a deep guttural bellow which shook the very core of the woodland and resonated off the trees.

With a loud last gasp of shock, his legs collapsed beneath him as the stag reared up and sent him staggering backward.

As he did so, he reached out with his arms to stop his fall and struck the barrel of the revolver onto a rock.

The last thing he saw was the huge Beast careering away just as the loaded barrel exploded violently in his horror-stricken face.

It was several weeks before his body was found. With injuries so severe that the corpse was unrecognizable, he was identified by the only thing he had on his person. The pocketbook. A paupers' burial in the woods by the Romany community was his destiny. William Thatcher had no family.

The Beast of Dragon Hill was never seen again and became nothing more than a local legend. Stanley, the horse, was stolen by a traveling salesman who, having retraced his steps searching for his lost notebook, could not believe his luck at finding an abandoned animal of such value and vanished without a trace.

The pointer dogs found their way back to the manor house after several days much to the bewilderment of the staff. The whereabouts of Sir Ieuan remained a much-conversed mystery among the local community and his family for many decades.

Presumed dead in a hunting accident, nobody made any concerted efforts to investigate further.

The commissioned painting was never completed and was found by a farmer among junk in an old barn some years later. Partially finished, the artist never painted the head, so above the shoulders were left a blank canvas. So the picture was incomplete and burned with the rest of the junk as worthless.

Flickering in flames, the farmer watched it burn and blister for half an hour before he noticed within the painting, the silhouette of a large stag stood on the horizon before a glorious red sunset.

DEAD HAUNTED COLLECTION

SHE SAW A GHOST

EXTRAORDINARY DEATH.

"The Coroner has held an inquest at Deepwynne touching the death of Dilys Ellen Mills, 17 years of age.

The girl had been in service at Fogmere. She spent a few days at home at Christmas and was then in her usual health. She came home unexpectedly on Saturday last and said she was not very well. On Sunday night, when in bed, she screamed and said she was frightened. Dr. Maddock, Brynafon, was summoned and attended. He found the deceased perfectly sensible. She could not speak but evidently understood what was said to her. She was making a noise half groaning and half screaming through her teeth, when he told her to stop the noise, she did so. She squeezed her eyelids closely together, but she relaxed them on his ordering her to do so. She was suffering from hysteria but was not in a severe state.

Death, however, occurred at half-past nine on Monday morning. Dr. Maddock, in his evidence, said that he was given to understand about a month ago the sailing ship Tradewind was lost, the brother of the girl's master at Fogmere House was the captain. Deceased heard a good deal about it, and on one occasion when she was left alone in the house she saw the shadow of a man on the blind. She took it to

> be the ghost of the captain of the Tradewind. That frightened her so much that her master and mistress would not get her out of her bedroom for a long time. Since then she has several times at night said she has seen the ghost. Those were delusions which would affect a girl in her state of health. She was practically bloodless.
>
> The mother of the girl said the deceased had several times told her that she had frequently seen a ghost standing by her bedside at night. Dr. Maddock gave as his opinion that having heard the history of the excitement from which the girl suffered, that she died in a fainting fit, brought on by excessive fright. In short, that she died from syncope. The jury returned the verdict accordingly."

For goodness sake. . .it was not supposed to happen like it did.

That damn foolish girl, I had to stop her. She would have revealed my secret and ruined everything. As if being killed at sea wasn't bad enough, I had to return to the house and cover up what I had done in the weeks leading to my death.

Who knew ghosts were real? Not me, indeed, I did not believe in the afterlife until. . .well, until I became one myself. How ironic, death has become me. All I am, all I represent now. So, I might as well make it the death I want, as there seems no end in sight.

Let me explain how it came to this unfortunate conclusion for the girl.

That cold November evening was a typical, bleak one. Freezing fog enveloped Fogmere House, and the gray sky threatened snow. I was staying at home for the foreseeable. However, I was expected to be grateful for the hospitality of the owners. My brother and his wife. The house should have been mine. Always the favorite son though, Peter had inherited the entire estate from our father ten years ago.

He was only the eldest son by about half an hour. We were twins. Growing up at Fogmere was a privilege. A grand house with fifteen bedrooms, a sizable oak-paneled hall with chandeliers and 100 acres of land which enjoyed a salmon river, and a beautiful lake which stretched out in front of the house, picturesque with its giant lily pads and black swans. We would spend hours riding our ponies around the grounds, laughing and swimming in the lake on hot summers days, not a care in the world. Not a single thought crossed my mind back then that one day this would all be his and none of this would be mine.

The parties at Fogmere in those early days were legendary. Grand dressy occasions would take place here in my father's prime. People would come from miles by invitation. Their horses and carriages attended to in the stable blocks by our grooms. The bedrooms would be prepared for guests by our housemaids, fires lit, decorated with fur blankets and fresh flowers and the downstairs would be a hive of activity as our staff strived to make everything perfect.

Peter and I would watch in awe from the galleried balcony above the main hall as lords and ladies would dance and engage in all their finery while staff hurried in and out with silver trays laden with vast amounts of canopies and expensive wines as the musicians played.

Our father was noticeably a wealthy man. The owner of a fleet of cargo ships, he imported many things, and so his wealth had brought him many friends in high places. One of whom caught my eye was a partner within the law firm my father uses and a wealthy owner of a string of elite gentlemen's clubs in London.

The typical playboy, Jones was a striking looking fellow with his glossy slicked black hair and dinner suits tailored by the top cloth houses. He smoked a pipe with the most excellent tobacco money could buy, and when I was just 14, he introduced me to the delirious temptation of the card game Poker, among other things.

At twenty-four - he was ten years our senior and Peter took an instant dislike to him. That night he beckoned us over after catching us observing a New Year's party well after midnight. We had wandered down the stairs and approached him tentatively. Upon checking our father was not looking and saw him laughing raucously in the corner with a small crowd of adoring guests hanging onto his every word.

We followed him into the drawing room where a group of men sat around a table, the smoke from their pipes filled the air, and through the dim light, we could see cards being dealt onto the table. I remember feeling in awe of how glamorous it was.

He handed us a glass each of amber liquid and laughed at our wide eyes.

"Time to show you boys what the real men do, hey?" he winked.

Peter choked on the Scotch, his eyes burning, and his tongue stuck out like he had been poisoned making the men burst out laughing much to his embarrassment. As the eyes focused on me next, I took a deep gulp, determined not to look at the fool and swallowed, however for me the warmth hitting the back of my throat was a delightful explosion to my senses, bringing me alive. Grinning, I raised the glass for more and the men cheered.

Ethan patted me on the back and said, "That's it, son. You will do well!" He winked at me, and I felt a glow of smug pride fill me.

Peter's face was still red, contorted as he held back from vomiting, his eyes stinging as he glared at me, unable to hide the sheer utter disgust on his face. But I felt elated. And from that moment on I admired the delectable Ethan Jones and delighted in his attention in the years that followed, as he groomed and shaped me into the playboy gambler I became. We became somewhat close, for we not only shared a love of the good life we also indulged in activities of the intimate kind.

As twins, Peter and I may have looked identical with our long blond, beautiful hair parted on the left and tied back, our blue eyes framed with blond lashed and fair skin. Both of us with tall, slim physiques and long fingers, we grew into handsome men. But our personalities were worlds apart.

Once we grew out of our boyhoods, when riding ponies and fishing, climbing trees and making dens no longer bonded us, my brother became boring. He was not interested in joining me on my trips to London. Instead, he became my father's right-hand man, and as our father ailed in his later years, he took over the Import business, working long hours late into the night in his study, pouring over the books.

Father made it very clear that he did not approve of my lifestyle and would make many a comment on how proud he was of Peter while shooting a glance of disdain my way. I didn't care for his approval anymore, and I did not mourn his passing.

Walking past the study as I did many a time at 3am, after a long evening of poker and brandy. I would see the glow of the lamp through the heavy wooden door, ajar just enough to see Peters face, strained and with his half-moon glasses perched on his nose as he dipped the nib of his pen into the inkwell. He would glance up at me, judgmental vibes radiating from his face and I would laugh before staggering to my bed. Who was having the most fun? Not him. He had forgotten how to smile. The only time I ever saw that poker face crack was on his wedding day. Oh yes, Peter married. Of course, he did. Perfect Peter! He married a dreary girl called Ellen, she was just as dull as he was. I thought how well suited they were. Ellen was worlds apart from the ladies and gentlemen that entertained us in London, now those were wild parties! I did nothing to hide my smirk whenever the memories of our debauched and lewd, drunken interludes popped into my mind.

Of course, when father died, he left it all to my brother. The house. The estate. The ships. Everything. He clarified it in his Will that I was not to have a penny, so much was his displeasure with me and how I had supposedly dragged the family name through the mud. Peter felt sorry for me, and although I resented his pity, I accepted the offer of continuing to live at Fogmere as I had been. It suited my lifestyle, and it impressed my social circle.

But I digress. I was telling you how it had come to this. Me, dead. . .and that senseless girl also dead.

One hot summers day, in July I had attended a poker game. This one was a little different, and Ethan had warned me this one would get intense. Perfect. I was more than ready for it. Some French clients of his were present, and basically, I lost everything that night. They were just too damn good players, and that night even my lover was out of his league. We gambled away every last penny we had, they bled us both dry. It took several days of sulking, hiding away getting drunk until we came up with a devious but fantastic plan.

An image of Peter came into my head. Sitting smug back at the Fogmere House with his perfect wife and perfect little family and I swore to get what was rightfully mine.

In the weeks that followed I had no choice but to return to Fogmere and confess all to him about my ill fortune. Word had got back to him before my return, tail between my legs, and he had a proposal waiting for me.

Peter asked me to charter a tramp steamer carrying the best Welsh coal over to several ports and collect large quantities of cotton, and sugar to return with. It would require several months at sea, bareboat with little crew, this would be a lucrative operation for us both. He assured me this assignment would be enough to clear my name and allow the debts I had built up to be settled, the graft would build up my stamina, and the money was excellent. He would pay me generously for this, as the consignment was a valuable one and he needed someone he could trust. Why that would be me, I cannot say, but I was in no position to question him. I needed the money, and this was going to help would help what I had planned with Ethan even more. To accept this offer meant that I could stay at Fogmere for a few weeks before the ship sailed, giving us plenty of time.

Peters wife Ellen had recently given birth to their third child. A baby boy named David that squawked and whinged way more than the other two brats had ever done. This meant that they were both tired. He had little sleep despite the employment of a wet nurse to give the exhausted parents rest, he still rarely got out of his bed until after 9am.

My late nights were limited too now that our shallow friends had all abandoned us, but this had given me the perfect excuse to play good boy, and to stay up late in the drawing room reading.

It was easy to pretend to be asleep by the fire in my armchair until I heard footsteps disappear up the stairs to his bed after midnight. Then I would slip into his study and carry out my plans with incredible care and attention so as not to cause any disturbance, making sure I replaced the pen back on its stand, after crossing the T's and dotting the I's.

Altering the figures and perfecting my brothers signature as Ethan had told me to. For six weeks, I moved money and shares into a separate account and smuggled various legal documents out where he would sign them, and I would return them to the files without disturbing so much as a feather pen. Peter would never know unless he had a good reason to check the documents and he was far too sleep deprived to pay them that much due diligence.

Legally the house would be mine when my dear brother's fraudulent activities would be exposed by the family's long-standing law firm for whom Ethan still had a partnership with, and he would be tried and hung for his crimes by the time I returned from sea. Being away ensured that I was out of the picture and gave me the perfect alibi while the trial took place, besides I had no desire to watch his pathetic wife simpering away in the courtroom either.

Everything was in place the day I set sail. The plan was that he would wait two weeks before alerting his partners to his concerns over a financial anomaly while doing the Fogmere accounts.

He was also to make a statement saying that Peter had blackmailed him into forging his father's will and there were several documents with his signature on them that would confirm a shifting of large sums of money out of client accounts into his own.

To top it all as a finishing touch, I had forged a letter thanking the French businessman for his "help" in fixing the poker game that ruined me and transferred a generous amount of money into his account. My own name would be cleared. The anticipated expressions of shock on people's faces when my brothers' crimes would be exposed made me smirk. How people would talk! Oh, what sweet revenge!

Ethan had ensured that the house would transfer into my name after Peters death and that his wife would inherit nothing. Now we could live in the house I deserved and live the lifestyle we both wanted. It was perfect...

...Until I died.

The storm on the third-night into the trip was insane. Out in the North Sea, there was little warning before the skies turned black and the first waves rocked my gigantic ship from side to side, tossing it about the vast dark sea like a leaf in the wind.

The rain had lashed our skin as I fought with the skeleton crew in vain to steady the vessel, being hurled from one side of the deck to the other. After my head had crashed into a metal pole, I realized with horror, that my own blood was spilling from the gash in my head. As it ran like a river down my face and into my mouth, mixed with the rain and the salt of the sea spray it tasted filthy. I dropped to the floor in a wretched heap, surrendering my broken body which went down with the ship to its watery grave.

It was like being sucked through a twister. . .death I mean.

Being shocked to my senses underwater as I roused from unconsciousness to find I was drowning filled me with an indescribable horror. Feeling my lungs fill with the salty water and the sting of the ice-cold water was shockingly painful as it closed over my head in a thunderous roar of vicious waves. My consciousness was dragged backward swirling, whirling, spinning around and around, and then something hit me.

It wasn't the sandy ocean floor though, oh no. This was the wall of Peter's study. Where I found myself looking down from the corner of the ceiling. Oddly, weirdly suspended in thin air, I was just there. And there I have stayed, lingering like a bad smell. Waiting. Waiting for something to happen, as it should have done. My consciousness had been so focused on this room and the contents of it, that this is where it returned immediately after my death.

As the hours ticked by I witnessed many things from that suspended position in the study.

One day I saw Peter blubbing. Sat at his desk, he suddenly sobbed into his blotting paper after a discussion with his wife about the ship still presumed *lost at sea*. Pathetic. If he cared that much for me, he should have done the decent thing and signed over half the house when our father died. Too late.

My interest peaked however when Ethan called at Fogmere House one afternoon in November. The butler, Grant, announced his arrival and was told to show him in. As tea was ordered and Grant left the room, Peter offered him a chair, and they talked.

Ethan offered his condolences as I listened intently. As the family lawyer, he explained how legally and financially he would need to arrange for anything in my name to be tied up, and I heard my brother clarify that I had nothing. I listened with bitterness as he explained how he couldn't trust me with anything because of my gambling habits.

Ethan's hands were sweating profusely by this point. His eyes darted around the office, and I knew he was wondering where I had hidden the paperwork. His body was held tight in the chair, and I heard him ask for a glass of water.

"Are you quite alright Sir?"

Enquired my brother, apparently confused at the state my love was presenting. I urged him silently to stay calm!

"Yes, I apologize. I must have eaten something disagreeable last night, some water would be helpful," continued he.

Peter rang the bell for Grant, but there was no response. The butler had disappeared downstairs to arrange for the tea tray, and the signal was missed. Rather than wait, Peter suspected poor Ethan was about to have a heart attack, so he stood up and said, "I will be right back, my good man, stay where you are." He left the room.

With no time to lose Ethan stood up, glancing nervously at the door where my brother had just exited, he hurried over to the desk and rifled through the drawers in desperation. His plan would be exposed should anyone find the documents I had altered, but it would still succeed if he could only modify details on the accounts and he planned to disappear with enough money to be comfortable. He would do anything. Anxiously muttering to himself he did not notice the young girl Dilys walk into the room.

Dilys was 17-years of age, and she had been in service at Fogmere for just two months. A strange girl, I had thought when I first met her I didn't like her prying eyes, they went everywhere like a terrible rash, and she seemed to drink in the surroundings of the elegant house and its plush furnishings like a cat that got the cream.

Her freckled face sported a sizable mouth which emphasized her small beady hazel eyes, which sat close together at the top of her piggy nose. She had a habit of lingering far too long when stoking the fire, I had noticed, to eavesdrop on family conversations and I had once walked into the bathroom in time to catch her stubby little hands fingering Mary's pearl necklace with a look of selfish desire on her face.

Now, the little brat was sneaking into the study, carrying a bucket of coal for the fire that did not need to be restocked, she apparently was curious to know what the meeting was all about. As she slid into the room, she suddenly stopped and stood, staring with her big mouth wide open at Ethan, her eyes absorbing the scene before her, and as he was desperately stuffing paperwork into his leather briefcase, she backed out of the room again quietly.

Damn!

That blasted girl had seen a golden opportunity to self-promote and get approval from her master. She hurried down the corridor, and I knew I had to do something. He must not be caught! I wanted him desperately to have what we had planned together, and my mind began to furiously work overtime. What could I do? Ethan was oblivious to the fact he was about to be rumbled and was still trying to gather up papers.

The rage inside me boiled. I stared hard at the heavy oak door and found myself there, going through it and following the girl. Something about her posture changed, and she stopped and turned around, stopping in her tracks, and she stared right through me. It was eerie. It took me by surprise, and I tried to speak to her, to yell at her and demand to know where she was going, but no sound came out.

When you are dead that tends to happen.

Dilys continued to walk down the long corridor, her pace quickening, it was with new urgency this time, and I sensed she felt my presence, not knowing what it was that was unsettling her. Her excitement and eagerness to tell her master about the intrusion of his guest had quickly turned to an uncanny feeling of being watched...followed.

I was right behind her.

Tapping her on the shoulder as hard as could, she stopped again. I was now confident that she felt that. She slowly turned back around, and although I was there, she still frustratingly could not see me. I was close enough to smell her breath. It was sweet and smelled of apples. She scratched her forehead in confusion, and I saw her physically shiver.

"Tsk!" she said with a shake of her head.

How DARE she dismiss me!? The arrogant little whore!

"TSK!" I replied, but this time, to my wicked delight, I saw her eyes widen with shock, and she backed into the wall slowly, her head anxiously swiveling all around her to see where that noise came from.

"TSK!" I said again.

She shrieked, and her hands flew to her mouth. Her face turned ashen, with the shock and her lips trembled. I had her exactly where I needed her to be, and with my new-found energy, fueled by the irritation burning my awareness, pushing a vase straight off a mahogany side table onto the floor, made Dilys scream in terror. Begging for mercy, she recited a prayer, and she clutched at the tiny cross that hung around her neck.

Then, finally, she looked at me. At once I knew she saw me.

The shadow she saw that day on the blind was me. After that moment, she ran, all the way to her bedroom where she hid under the blankets shaking violently with terror. I followed, hounding her night and day until she died. I did not leave her side. I did not allow her to sleep. If she closed her eyes, I would prod her. The evil whisper deep into her ear, tug at her clothes and tap on things was me. And it was relentless until the wretched girl gave up.

Ethan got away, making his excuses he politely declined the tea when Peter returned leaving him standing baffled as he tipped his hat and bid him a good day.

That should have been the end of the story. My beloved Ethan should be sitting comfortably in the armchair by the fire at Fogmere House, with me in spirit watching over him, finally, perhaps my spirit could have rested, witnessing the demise of pathetic Peter and I would have watched with pleasure as he lost Fogmere House.

Several weeks after the death of Dilys, there was a knock at the front door of Fogmere. Grant answered and sheepishly showed in two members of father's law firm. Ethan was not among them. With solemn faces they were shown into the office and right away their conversation turned grim. I learned how he had approached them as he had planned with anomalies in the paperwork. One partner, a Mr. Cecil Smyth however, was meticulous in his forensic accounting and had burned the midnight oil for several days poring over the books.

Ethan had clearly had no time at all to double check my alterations and having handed the papers over, Cecil must have noted an uncharacteristic look of nervousness in his eyes. He found an important document that I had clumsily overlooked, and unfortunately, Peter was able to testify that indeed these signatures were forged, providing an alibi for dates that our father could not possibly have been present for and noting a date on one document signed by father *after* his death. Hell, and Damnation! The brandy in my brain had not favored me with focus and clarity during those late nights.

My wish to be with my beloved in the end was not granted. He joined me in death briefly after he was hanged for his crime of fraud but was dragged away by a wailing black shadow figure, probably to his own place of retribution wherever that may be.

Ironically Peter and his family have all moved on after death I never saw any of them again, and his eldest son inherited the property. He was just as uninteresting as his father and didn't hold any interesting parties. Today I wander the many rooms of Fogmere House. I still sometimes see the irritating freckled girl snooping through visitors' things, and when she sees me, she vanishes.

I will never stop watching the house and its guests. Every now and then I will show my disproval at building works planned that I disapprove of by breaking something. Occasionally, if a guest has been obnoxious, I will make sure he or she gets a fright by standing over them in their sleep and wake them with my ice-cold breath.

Fogmere House is mine and mine it shall remain.

DEAD HAUNTED COLLECTION

THE WITCH OF YNYS PENGLOG

A few miles off the Penwynshire Coast is where the rugged coastline of Welsh island Ynys Penglog begins. Its craggy shores bite into the salty ocean water and provide a home for rare seabirds, like puffins and Manx.

Few human inhabitants are tough enough to survive there. However, this tale began when the island contained but a single dweller, an old woman named Winny Madog.

Those on the mainland supposed she was a witch. She took the appearance of one. Winny would walk doubled over with her wild hair which, white as the bubbling seafoam, raged around her body and draped down to the floor as she walked. Wearing rags, dense and dark in color, she tied her skirt around her ankles to allow her free movement across the rocky shores, and her feet were bare, the soles thick and impenetrable like rawhide.

But her eyes. . .they were intense bright blue, and they could see further over the sea than most. The old woman seldom voyaged to the mainland. Only when she required food desperately and could not manage with what the island provided would she venture there. Who she was and how she came to live there though, nobody knew, and her mystery made people distrust her all the more.

Rumours abounded that she arrived on the island after a massive storm and was regurgitated by the sea onto the rocks. Some had tried to interrogate her about this, but each time she was confronted, no response would ever be returned except a deep stare with those icy blue eyes, followed by a terrific storm in the hours that followed.

Weirdly the witch was only ever seen skulking near the mainland just before inclement weather. This added fuel to the talk she could incite a storm whenever she desired, cursing the mainland folk, taking the lives of innocent fishermen, and people feared her visits. Not wishing to upset the old hag, they would serve her the goods that she would point at with a knarled finger. Without speaking she would exchange freshly caught fish, her currency, for supplies like grain and salt. Those individuals would breathe out in relief when she had left, for to upset the evil sorceress would mean your family was fated to suffer a loss in the storm, which would soon come.

Winny had fashioned a crude habitation out of one cave, and as the years passed, she showed no intention of leaving. Most of the time she spent her day's collecting things that had washed up on the shoreline, as well as cooking and fishing. Using the gifts the sea brought her with the tides, she was never short of fishing nets. It would take her hours to untangle and repair them. Winny had learned an efficient system which involved wading out into the icy waters in the late evenings to cast out the nets, fixing them to an old shipwreck and a haggard tree that grew out of the rocks. In the mornings, there would be a bounty of fish, crabs, and sea life decorating the nets. In the spring and summer months, time was spent digging a small herb and vegetable patch laboriously with just her bare, gnarled hands and a splint shaped stone. Strong as an Ox the old woman could drag enormous lumps of driftwood for her fire and could lift rocks to build herself shelters and storage for her food.

Unremitting was the harsh routine of living on the island, and the bird population would sit like companions waiting for her to throw them fish guts and small fry. She took nothing from the island that was more than she needed. If a bird were sick, Winny would keep it in a fisherman's cage until it regained strength, healing broken wings and other injuries whenever she could. They seemed to respect she was at one with them and reimbursed her kindness by dropping a rainbow variety of feathers for her to add to a curtain of strange dangling ornamental charms, woven with shells, seaweed, and twine. In the breeze, the shells would catch the wind and the collection together formed an eerie chorus of whistles and rattles. As the feathers quivered, the shells played tunes with every flurry, and Winny could forecast the weather instantaneously.

Winny knew the locals were suspicious of her, but she did not care to correct them. She would take a small boat, another one of the donations the sea had gifted her if she needed necessary provisions but made no eye contact with anyone and would scurry by the gossiping womenfolk and disregard the youths who mocked her.

Had Winny perished in the cave-dwelling, not a soul would have noticed, until the visits to the mainland ceased altogether. That, or had there been the absence of dim lamplight on stormy nights, for those nights were the only ones the frugal old woman ever lit one. Hence the ominous glow of light from the cave-dwelling was taken as a definite sign that impending storms were to come.

"Hey!" twelve-year-old Tom Jenkins yelled across to her one day. "Old woman is it true you be the Witch of Ynys Penglog island?"

He mocked, to the delight of his sniggering cronies. But she had not flinched. Her face poker-straight as she continued her mission to get what she needed to be done and return to the haven of her isle.

The youth continued to bellow obscenities at Winny before his mother, Mo, came out of one of the small houses to see what all the fuss was about. When she saw Winny, she clipped him over the ear with a sharp hand and sent him scurrying.

That dark, gloomy night the sky looked ominous, black clouds began to gather, the sunset was cloaked by the swirls of doom, and as evening drew in the waves started to boom furiously against the rocks. Two fishermen stood on the cliffs on the mainland looking over the vast dark ocean. Storm clouds were creeping across the horizon creating a feeling of impending doom.

"A storm is brewing," one said.

They pondered a few moments before the other replied, "Aye, we are in for a wild night, so we are. Let's hope no boats are out tonight, or they for sure will be dashed to pieces on the rocks."

The first man replied, "Aye man, the old witch woman has been ashore this afternoon. She is often seen as the curse of bad weather, there is no good about the old hag, and we have her to thank for those that sleep beneath the waves I'm sure."

Nodding in agreement his mate replied, "Pray to God she has not cast her curse on anyone tonight!" They stood to stare out to sea and shuddered.

Suddenly a light glinted across the water, and the men exchanged glances as they realized it would be Winny's lamp lit.

"Most folks know to avoid her, but young Tom was mocking her this aft. No doubt he got the curse for that. . .now do you hear that wind? We need to shelter!"

The men turned and began to walk toward the hamlet in which they lived as the heavens opened and huge raindrops started to fall, only to be met by a frantic looking woman.

"Have you seen my husband?" her voice cried desperately. It was Toms mother, Mo Jenkins. Her dark hair was stuffed into a cloth bonnet tied firmly under her chin, brown eyes wide and skin pale, she hugged a black shawl around her shoulders. The men shook their heads, "Has the Hag lit her lamp?" she continued, to which the men nodded solemnly.

"Yes. . .it's going to be a bad storm! You can't go yonder looking for your husband ma'am! It isn't safe, the waves are almost reaching the top of the cliffs already!"

Frantic the woman paid no heed to the men's instruction and continued up the path toward the cliff tops. When she reached the top, breathless by now, the wind and rain were lashing down in torrential force, soaking her to the skin. Standing staring out into the blackness of the ocean, her long skirts weighed heavy with the burden of rainwater. Mo's husband Dai had not returned with his fishing boat yet. He was out there now, at the mercy of the curse of the wicked old woman whom Mo felt for sure, had placed a curse on them thanks to their sons wayward taunting earlier.

Winny's lamp was visible across the water like a glow worm, a flicker in the infinite black abyss of roaring winds. Seawater spray stung Mo's eyes, and she could hardly hear herself speak as she began to say the Lord's prayer, quietly building up emotion until she was begging God for mercy upon her husband. Afterward, exhausted, she stood for an hour just staring at the light, plainly visible through the sheet of rain and wondered about it. Was the witch trying to lure the fisherman to her lair?

As the rain continued to infiltrate her trembling skin, Mo no longer cared about getting drenched. She could feel the aggressiveness of the wind pushing her toward the edge of the cliff, her clothes now so waterlogged they dragged her downwards. One step closer would plummet her to a grisly death, where she could join her beloved Dai. She pictured their flesh rotting, hair swirling around them, their eyes staring and cold through the water...it snapped her to her senses.

Mo knew that she could not stand in this place long before being swept out to sea herself. As a mother duty kicked in and she was forced to retreat to her home, to Tom and her other four children. She had no choice but to resign and wait for the storm to pass. She expected the sea to posset out the corpse of her husband days later. With hopelessness weighing heavily on her soul she headed home.

Back home, Winny was crouched by a small fire in her little cave when she heard the terrified scream of a man's voice above the thunderous roar of the storm.

She lit her lantern, threw a blanket over her hunched back and carried it to the mouth of her dwelling. Through the thunder of the waves and howling unforgiving wind, Winny could make out the dark shape of a man on the rocks where the sea had violently hurled him. His bulk of a body had been tossed onto the cliffs outside her cave where it lay broken and torn, about 20 feet away from her.

The groaning man squirmed...she did not stop and stare, nor did she dawdle. Gathering her shawl, she worked it under the crushed body. With one hand outstretched she used all her strength to drag the victim toward the safety of her cave, where the glow of the fire inside was a welcome beacon from the lashing waves.

Once inside she swiftly and silently got to work, throwing a thick woolen blanket over his limp, bleeding body and stoking the fire. Fetching water, herbs, and rags Winnie worked to dress the raw gaping wounds of the injured man who was passing in and out of awareness. His hands were bloodied, and he had several deep cuts to his face and head. Winny did not meet his dark and desperate eyes with her own. Toiling through the night, bathing his head and administering her herbal concoction to the patient, who eventually passed out from the pain.

In the morning the quiet sunrise and call of the seabirds signaled the end of the storm. As Dai Jenkins awoke, he did not know where he was for several long and painful moments. He groaned in agony as he slowly sat up and gathered his senses. Looking down at his dressed wounds, seaweed poultices were carefully tied with twine around his feet and arms, a warm blanket wrapped around him. The sun streamed through the entrance to the cave, and the white feather curtain gently swayed and chimed, catching glints of rock crystal that cast rainbows all around him. Realizing his life had been saved, at last, he looked around for Winey to thank her, but she was nowhere to be seen.

Several days passed. Winny never spoke to Dai, but she would appear regularly and redress his wounds. She would bring him hot fish broth and herb tea to sip. Dai tried to talk to her, but she merely carried about her business and did not answer. One day, when he could stand tentatively on his feet, she stood at the mouth of the cave indicating with a nod and a grunt and her outstretched arm to the direction of the shore.

Dai understood, and he graciously left, thanking her profusely for her kindness and found her small boat tethered waiting for him to make the journey home across the now calm sea.

A small crowd had gathered on the shore of the mainland by the time the tiny boat reached the coast. Some children had seen the approaching vessel, called out to their parents and word had quickly spread. Men waded out and helped Dai to shore, supporting him on their shoulders and called for Mo to be fetched at once. How they rejoiced as Mo embraced him with tears and hugs, Tom and the other children dancing around him with a thousand questions. As Tom regaled the gathering with his story of how the old woman had saved his life, they listened with disbelief and shock, news traveled widely across the land of her good deed.

After that day Winny was heralded by the local people who no longer mocked or taunted her. But they still believed fervently that she was a witch. The light that shone on storm days was the magic she used to enchant the sea into bringing her what she needed. Her knowledge of healing was nothing short of sorcery, and the herb poultices were studied with great interest by the local doctor who declared them to be of witchcraft origin.

From that day, various offerings of food were delivered by fishermen to the island for Winny and gifts of firewood, blankets, clothing, and food from the women often was left for her. Her reputation was still feared. However, there was reverence now, that her presence was to be respected.

The sight of Winny's lamp lit at the beginning of a storm was no longer seen as a terrible omen. Instead, it was a beacon of hope that the sea might provide unlucky fishermen with safety. When one day the goods they had left remained untouched the locals knew she was dead. Her body, however, was never found.

To this day on a squally night, from the cliff tops on the mainland, the faint glow of light can be seen emanating from the cave where she once lived. Many fishermen account that they have heard the eerie sounds of whistling on the sea long before the wind picks up, and white feathers will land around them warning them of a storm to come.

DEAD HAUNTED COLLECTION

THE GAMEKEEPER

> Evening Express 10th June 1898
> **MURDER AT MARSHAM - HORRIBLE DEATH OF A GAMEKEEPER.**
>
> His Body Found Mutilated in the Park. The neighbourhood of Marsham and Port Talgat was thrown all Friday morning into a state of intense excitement by the news of a terrible murder on Miss Talgat's estate. A gamekeeper, named Ascott, well known, was found early in the morning brutally murdered in the park. The unfortunate man had been shot, and afterwards terribly battered, apparently with a bludgeon or the butt end of a gun. There were evidences of a desperate struggle nearby, and it is surmised the keeper, who was known to have enemies amongst the poaching fraternity, surprised some men during the night, and was murdered.

It was a comfort to find myself secure lodgings after my misery the recent few years. I had served in the British Army which had taken its toll on my health and as the outcome; I had received a severe public flogging as the penance for desertion.

I had elected to stow away from my base in Malta and return to Wales. Worth every laceration on my back. Every drop of blood I shed released a relief. I was comfortable with the pain you see. My dirty blond hair had become long and mingled with a beard yet indeed this could not conceal my sea weathered skin and the great tumours in my neck. I sick repeatedly.

A spasm in my skull would grab me by surprise when I was least expecting it, appearing as if a serpent was twisted round under my throat and round the opposite side of the head and coiled on the upper part of my brain. The knowledge of all the horrors I had been witness to in the last few years, I assumed had morphed into these visible lumps and excruciating pains.

I felt more restored by those 12 strikes of the cat-o'-nine-tails than ever. Shame the sense didn't last, and I had to resort to stabbing my hands with pins whenever I was left behind only with my anguished thoughts for any quantity of time.

My fingers were red raw and full of scabs from this habit but care I did not. My parents could not grant me sanctuary, and I would not burden them. The shame of having a son convicted of desertion was sufficient to send them to a premature grave, they did not deserve that. My father had given me the benefit of learning, a luxury most could not afford. But I, unlike most, could read and write effectively. For that I remained eternally indebted. The snatched moments when I could emerge myself between the pages of a novel or newspaper were solitude and refuge. No value could be given upon those during those bleak periods in India. Yet he regarded, quite accurately, that I had let him down and he was ashamed of me.

I could not foresee them to accept why I did what I did. I realized the humiliation and dishonor I had bestowed on the family name being enough to keep me from darkening their door.

Mother occasionally met me in secret away from the prying eyes of village gossips and the tittle-tattle of folk in a churchyard where she tended to the graves. She cared for me and wished me safe, but her heart was weak, she had frequent faint episodes and seldom spoke aloud to anybody anymore.

I informed her of the James couple advertising for a lodger. She looked alarmed and urged me to take care, for Harry James, a convicted poacher was notorious.

"Son, should you require anything at all ask for Tom Pepper in the next village? His wife Hannah is a good sort. She will get a message to me. Keep your nose clean my lad and you'll soon be right when all this scandal is forgotten," she responded.

I approached the narrow terrace house at the end of the street that backed on to farmland and stopped. No worldly possessions to my name, though mother had provided me enough coins to afford me a half week of the board, and after that, well I had nothing else to barter with but the assurance of the honest graft.

I knocked on the door. It was eventually answered by a small woman with beady grey eyes, stout and squat, with brown curled hair framing a sweaty brow. A broom in one hand onto which she leaned against, she squinted through a four-inch gap with which the access was secured by a chain, and panted like a dog. I imagined it wouldn't take considerable exercise for her to reach a state of exhaustion.

"Can I help you?" she snarled in Welsh, somewhat aggressively.

Eyeing me with uncertainty, she did not release the door to be entirely opened until I held out the coins in my palm and enquired after lodgings.

When she noticed the money her attitude changed suddenly, and she closed the door again for a second as she drew the chain free. She heaved the entrance wide and yelled behind her.

"Harry! Lodger!"

She ushered me through to a small front room. It was sparsely furnished with a wooden table and three chairs.

"Sit!" she barked.

This woman commanded obedience, and I was glad to oblige. After several years in the army, I was used to receiving orders. She was as foreboding as any sergeant.

She shut the door, and the place darkened. She shuffled through the cramped hallway into a gloomy passageway and I overheard the mumble of voices as I glanced around me.

The accommodation was simple. A substantial iron stove occupied one wall with blazing coals and a pot on the boil . A savoury smell warmed my nostrils, and suddenly I felt ravenous. On a stone slab in the corner, I observed a pile of bloodstained feathers. Pheasant stew I guessed.

"HARRY JAMES!"

Boomed a voice with a rich Welsh accent ending my thoughts of a tasty broth abruptly. I swivelled around, standing to attention, addressing the towering, muscular dark fellow who stood before me. His solid jawline and heavy black eyebrows framed an extremely fierce looking stare, so I avoided making full eye contact with him as I outstretched my hand to shake his. I noticed deep scars on his arms as he hesitated then reluctantly reached out giving me a hard grip.

"Joe Lewellyn, please to make your acquaintance sir," he then ignored me and strode to the stove.

"Three shillings a week, includes a meal once a day and you work with me," Harry James declared.

His voice hard and precise.

"Thank you, Sir. Very kind, Sir," I echoed, I was Incredibly grateful.

Harry's eyes studied me up and down, and his focus on my pin-pricked hands caused me to place them self-consciously into my pockets.

"I don't ask no questions. So, don't expect any either. You got that boy?"

It was a statement, not an inquiry.

We nodded in unison, and we came to an implied understanding that day. He picked up some tin bowls from a ledge and handed them to his spouse. She filled them with steaming broth from the pot and offered me one.

With a grateful smile we sat to eat, and I believed things would be all right here.

As the weeks passed, I grew to respect my new landlord and landlady very much. My bed, a narrow wooden pallet with blankets, and a straw mattress, was more comfortable than any alternative place I had bedded down in. A timber cross hung above the bed, besides it a window through which the mountain was visible.

In the evenings I lay down with a candle lit, reading. They did not have books, but Harry James kept an eager eye on the local newspapers.

I could hear owls screeching as they hunted in the adjacent woods. I fought sleep, because with the darkness nightmares came. As my eyes closed, hallucinations of gunshots, splattered blood, men screaming and terror...agony and acts of torture would infest my brain.

I would wake in a sweat, shouting out for mercy and sit upright in the dark disorientated and gasping for breath, then start shaking and weeping until I began to see dawn break again, thus I'd remember. I was safe.

Mornings were different from those in India and Malta. The sunlight glowed unlike it does overseas. More yellow tones than crimson, and no fierce heat only a refreshing breeze. It was early summer in Wales, and a steady stream of light flooding through the window early morning brought an amnesty from the darkness and the harmony of birds singing and sheep calling was a symphony to my ears.

Harry and his wife, Em, never brought up my nocturnal disturbances. They must have heard me for at times I knew I had yelled so loud the roof above me shook. But it wasn't discussed, and for that I was thankful. True to his word, no questions asked.

In regard of this I did not question either, so every weeknight I would put on the dark coat and hat given to me by Em and follow Harry out of the house into the darkness. Gratified with a belly full of decent food, we would hike up the lane to the farm behind us and prepare for a night of rustling. We would meet in an old outbuilding, some three miles north of the farm in a field with other men and dogs, frequently six or seven of them. Here tools of the trade, shot and snares, would be swapped and tokens of information swapped in hushed tones.

No light being used, and I would shadow Harry like a hound. Following a path trod many times before, he knew every rabbit hole and rock because blindfolded by night, and with only the stars on a clear evening to show the way, we had to rely on our senses entirely.

Griffiths, the proprietor of Bryntagleth Farm where we would meet, would regularly appear upon us at the gate and tip his hat to Harry. There was an understanding. I gathered from the meetings, that these poachers were granted admittance to the property because of the vermin they kept under control in exchange.

A foxtail or a mole would be nailed to the gate on our return, to appease Griffiths and in turn, he authorized them to use his land. The reason for this became evident to me quickly. The poachers didn't wish to pilfer his farmland, even though there were acres and acres of it. Oh no. They didn't wish for just hares and rabbits. They wanted ACCESS! Access to the countryside behind the farm. Private property. The territory of the local gentry and that of Marsham Castle. Land with deer, pheasant and much valued game.

Marsham Castle was occupied by Lady Clarence Talgat. Inherited from her father, she split her time between residences in London and in Wales. The owner of most of the properties in the county she was a favorite member of society, respected and adored by local folk. Her estate was vast, with a deer park and maintained by her extremely well paid and esteemed gamekeepers.

One warm July evening, at twilight I followed Harry to the stone barn for the nights poaching as normal but his mood that daytime was sombre. He carried weight in his mind and had uttered very few words all day. Not that extraordinary for him, but I noticed Em had been on eggshells around him as well. I sensed something troubling him. It didn't take long to discover what that was. He met with Maddox and Thomas, two dirty looking poachers that were regulars at our meets.

"They 'ave for sure gone down Arry," said Maddox. He was a gaunt man, with patchy grey facial hair and a squint. As he spoke he eyed Harry with greed, with this sly dig. Clearly, he had a hankering for provocation. He was hoping for a reaction from this remark, and evidently, he knew something did not about what was bothering Harry.

"Ay. That bloody bastard Ascott. I swear to God I'm gonna blow his BRAINS out one of these days!"

Harry rarely trembled as he spoke, unusually with restrained and brooding anger that I hadn't seen before although I recognised him to be capable of it.

Oh yes. Men like him I had involvement of in the army. The most dangerous men I knew were superficially calm. Seldom did they exhibit any hint of losing control, and yet once the shootings started... the bloodlust was unleashed. I saw men kill others for killing's sake, the taking of lives to release pent-up aggression, was to them, no more of a question than as if scratching an itch.

Maddox looked delighted.

Thomas glanced at me and subsequently, as we lay down low by a stone wall watching for pheasant, he informed me what I had suspected. Two of Harry's associates had been caught poaching and were to be sentenced. Ascott was the chief gamekeeper for Marsham Castle, and he and Harry had a history.

Harry once served a months tough labor once after being caught red-handed on the Castle grounds with a rifle a few seasons ago. Harrys attempts to pay off the keeper with money had didn't persuade him, Ascott being famed for his integrity, and James had sworn vengeance upon the fellow who had committed the evidence to convict him.

The atmosphere from that day remained heavy with a dark sense of foreboding. I realized something was brewing with Harry, but it was none of my business.

My nose was as clean as my poverty would support, for any cleaner and I would starve to death.

Poaching was a means to eating and sleeping between the night terrors and was my only reality. Besides, as rural crimes go it was rife, and I wasn't doing anything that most other men in my position would not do. Many turned a blind eye to it.

After the life I had suffered, it was just a way to exist. It seemed to me, more immoral that all around us people were living with a lack of food and yet there on the doorstep lay this rich land, rich with produce and game to satisfy the already fat gentry. I thanked the lord often for his blessing and saw that if I held my head down for a few more years until the shame of my desertion faded, then luck might find me a more honest path.

When John Jenkins from the village visited by one afternoon to lend Harry his rifle, I took surprisingly little note. Harry had enough of his own rifles, and I could see no reason for this transaction except that Jenkins gun was a better modern double barrel. I expected perhaps Harry may be considering acquiring one for himself?

That evening though, June 9th was a particularly blustery day. When the wind was up, poaching opportunity was good as gunshot noise was less likely to be heard. But Harry had an odd request. He wished to go fishing instead, and he told Em he would be gone all night. She did little to query her husband, she never did. I caught her give him a knowing glance and nodded to me.

"Take him fishing wi' you Har. the water is up on the river after all the rainfall".

That night we took a sack complete with nets and bait. Em packed up thick cornbread, and cold meat packed in paper and string and Harry filled his hip flask with brandy.

We set out at seven o'clock, the sun was veiled by dark clouds, and the wind blew a chill enough to give me goosebumps. Walking towards the river would have taken us west up the lane, but Harry kept walking toward Bryntagleth Farm–our usual poaching route.

"Hey, the river is this way?!"

I had observed, assuming he maybe was on autopilot.

He grunted and continued on the track.

Knowing better than to argue I followed and after unloading the fishing gear at the gate to the field which leads up the mountain towards the Marsham Estate, I knew then something was going to happen. I trailed Harry for about two miles across the area. Instead of using stone walls to cloak us from the view of anybody that might have been using a field glass he remained in clear sight by hiking through the midst of the fields as did I. Thankful for small mercies, I was not afraid of being shot at, it was public knowledge that Lady Talgat did not allow her men to carry guns. At this point, however, I had no notion as to what Harry was playing at.

Sure enough, we quickly caught a voice cry from a distance away. Stopping we looked around us and below in the field we observed three men approaching.

"HEY!!! YOU! STOP!" came the voice.

We ran to an adjacent stone wall and squatted down on the floor panting from the exertion.

"Do as I say Lewellyn," said Harry.

I nodded, still entirely uncertain about what he was doing, but by now positive that it was no accident that we had been caught trespassing.

"STAY THERE!" he said.

With that, he ran, hunched low along the wall about 20 yards and gestured to beckon me. I followed. He reached back the thickets covering the stones and dragged out the double-barrel shotgun from Sam Davies that had been concealed within the rocks. A long, hard glare at me broke my gasp from becoming words. The men were closing in on us.

We kept still. The wind blew strong, it was difficult to hear anything around that might have given away that a man was on the other side of that wall. Harry gave me a nudge and signalled with his head for me to stand up and look. As I did, he loaded the gun.

Slowly, I rose.

The moment my eyes locked with his, it was impossible to express which of us was more shocked. Me or that of the gamekeeper I found out subsequently to be Robin Ascott.

"DON'T SHOOT!"

Ascott spoke with a thick Scottish accent, as he put both hands in the air, plainly startled to meet me at such proximity.

I raised both my arms up to prove to him I too was unarmed.

BANG!

My eyes locked as my face was splattered with his blood.

The effect was awful. The unfortunate man's right cheek was turned towards the gun, and the mere force of the explosion at such close range dislocated his lower jaw. The charge, entering his right cheek, shattered the whole of his face tearing flesh and skin, and splintering the nasal bones spattering the wall with blots of blood.

Blinded, choked by the blood, shattered teeth and splintered bone which filled his mangled mouth, the victim fell back.

But he was not dead yet.

Staggering to his knees he crawled onwards, for some fifteen yards, pitching for ward, rising again on hands and knees. But just as he got in front of the second gap his desperate strength failed him, and he sank back against the bank.

It all happened in such a blur after that.

Harry pushed through the gap in the wall and ordered me to follow.

He reached the bleeding Ascott and raised the barrels of the gun once more.

"STOP!" I shouted in vain as the second blast fired at close range into the victims right shoulder; the flame burnt the cloth of his coat and singed his hair. The shot tore a hole in his shoulder, and carried the coat sleeve away.

That finished the ghastly work.

With the words, "Dead men tell no tales!" Harry unleashed a savage eruption of violence at the wretched man and began to boot him about the head over and over. Swearing at him and brutally clubbing what little remained of his skull with the butt of his gun until he had sapped his strength and thus he settled back panting. Surveying his murder with a sneer, we heard the shouts of the other men in the distance calling out Ascott's name.

I was in such distress I did what I do best.

I bolted.

At that moment I did not care if Harry shot me in the back. I preferred to die anyhow. Sick of witnessing the slaughter, death, and brutal massacre of my fellows. I broke and flew not knowing where the hell I was going.

I stumbled across the fields and continued running until my chest burned. Tears stung my eyes, and my throat swelled up so tight that the air could scarcely escape. When I came to a barn, I hid inside and wedged into a corner where I broke down. Crying and convulsing, digging at my fists until they oozed blood, I longed for that flogging to take place again right now. I craved to go through pain like I had never before, to discharge the venom in my mind. I felt polluted.

I lingered in that barn until dusk fell. By this point, I had steadied down sufficiently to think and I recalled my mother's words.

Find Tom Pepper.

What Tom Pepper was going to achieve for me I had no concept, but logic wasn't an option. I just remember thinking how I could not bear my mother and father to believe their son was a murderer, and I had to get a message to them that I was innocent before getting as far away as feasible.

I lumbered down the lane and kept wandering in a daze towards the glowing lights of the village where he lived. Stopping on the way, I saw a man stood swaying by a gatepost, clinging to a bottle. I quizzed him as to where Tom Pepper was, and he gave me slurred directions to a modest cottage 100 yards away.

Thank GOD.

I knocked on the door, and it was opened by a tall man with long blond hair and a beard. He wore a maroon scarf around his neck and was smoking a pipe. It wasn't until I saw the switch in his expression when he glanced down at my clothes that I understood I was covered in blood.

"I...I am Joe Lewellyn," I said.

His face dawned and almost as if he was expecting me he ushered me into the house where his wife was seated sewing by a fire.

I wish I hadn't involved them that night. Good folk, respectable people that did not merit to have my troubles brought to the door. They asked no questions, they just listened as I blurted out over and over what had transpired, with a wide-eyed look of dismay.

"I didn't do it I swear I didn't kill him."

> EVENING EXPRESS 11TH JUNE 1898
> **THE MURDERER S MOTIVE.**
> In searching for the murderer the police are looking for a man with a motive. That is to say, their circle of suspicion is narrowed by the very plausible theory that the motive for the deed must have been greater than a chance Poacher's endeavour to escape detection by the keeper. No man would put his neck in a noose or commit a crime of such cold-blooded malice for the sake of escaping punishment for a comparatively trivial offence. It is, therefore, considered certain that the murderer and his victim had met before, under circumstances which bred an intense hatred on the murderer's side. Ascott had determined enemies amongst the poaching class, though he was held in high esteem by the villagers and by the men under him.

I was stunned to learn that they arrested Harry James the following day. It turned out he had been rather publicly verbal in his threats towards Ascott's life and he was the first man people suspected. I knew it was merely a matter of time before they showed up for me as well.

Tired of running away. Sick of hiding and living with nightmares I just accepted my fate. An eerie calmness set in, and it was the first time in years that I had felt resigned to my destiny.

The crowds lined the streets the day we were all taken to the court for trial.

James, Tom Pepper and his wife (for being accessories and hiding me) and me. The people were wild. They jeered and hollered, scoffed and chanted obscenities at us as we were driven in the omnibus through the town to hear the judge consider the crime of murder. Then rotten fruit was hurled at us, and they stood on coal wagons to obtain a better view.

> SOUTH WALES ECHO 20th June 1898
> **MARSHAM MURDER. PRISONERS BEFORE THE MAGISTRATES. FOUR PERSONS IN THE DOCK.**
> Harry James Discharged. It would appear as though public interest in the Marsham tragedy increases rather than diminishes. This morning the approaches to the Port Talbot station were thronged by hundreds of interested spectators. Coal trucks were utilised as stands by men and boys, and almost the whole of the route from the railway station to the Police Court was lined with onlookers.

What I didn't foresee was the lies from Harry James. After we had traveled together in the cart, he had spoken to me in Welsh about how he was going to get us both off, how he had witnesses that would give us an alibi.

But later he stood up in court and stated to the jury that he had been out fishing that evening and sure enough he produced a credible eyewitness. There were so many witness statements. Thirty maybe or forty people, eager to be involved in the most notorious murder in their lifetime and savouring the celebrated attention it brought them.

Most were dismissed as mere hearsay. Individuals who alleged they had seen me that day, people with whom I never even passed the time of day. One guy said they had seen me with a gun. Another had seen me near the estate about an hour before the murder. James claimed that on the train I had confessed to the murder and informed him where I had stashed the murder weapon. The witness to this exchange was a warden who indeed confirmed we had been speaking, but as he could not speak Welsh, he didn't know what was said. I could cross-examine James myself, but my attempts were futile. He had an alibi and a solicitor that got him discharged without further questioning.

Then arrived the sting. The farmer we met on a regular basis claimed that I had confessed the murder to him. As he delivered his carefully rehearsed speech, a gasp resonated from the gathered spectators in the courthouse. He was so convincing in his manner. So undoubted. My world crashed to the dock at that point, and I realized this was the final nail in my coffin.

I pleaded not guilty.

A cheer roared as I was condemned for the murder of Robin Ascott. Public satisfied that justice had been done. I hung my head and quietly accepted my circumstance as the death sentence was announced.

Once inside the cell, I was left solely with my thoughts. The worst punishment I could get was not death, it was solitary confinement. The days and nights merged into one long agonizing wait, and there was no natural light in my cell. Sitting on a cold stone slab waiting for death was when I began to notice him.

Trying to remain awake, and not go through the misery of sleep for the hallucinations and persecution it would lead me to, I turned on my side and stared at the back of the iron door.

I was struggling not to listen to the wails of misery and insanity. Cries of pain, screams of rage and abuse, reverberated and ricocheted from all aspects. The jangling of chains, grinding metal and slamming doors intermingled with howling, swearing, thudding and other indescribable sounds that were savage. Demonic sounding.

If sleep were to win over, I would simply see and hear the same things just I would be continuing in it, observing my fellow officers being decapitated, executed and burned alive.

The choice I had was grim.

As I lay down in the murky corner of the cell, the concentration of my focus slowly built up as I saw him standing there.

Robin Ascott.

His face was hanging, bloodied, savaged and torn. The left eye over his shattered skull was concentrated on me, and his handlebar mustache was perfect on one side alone. The other side...there was an empty shell where the rest of his face had been blasted away. The shadows in the room cast uncertainty on what I was witnessing.

Shutting my eyes did nothing to erase him from my view, I felt him even more.

My heart started to thump in my rib cage, and I felt the swell in my neck start to constrict. I screamed out

"Ascott..." the pitiful sound my voice made was swamped out by the commotion.

I sat upright.

Ascott gaped.

I felt his eyes bore down into my conscience and I struggled to communicate to him. I don't consider he was angry with me.

He merely stood there. He didn't move, he didn't make a sound. He just glared.

The hours passed and neither of us moved an inch until daylight when a prison guard entered the chamber bearing letters. He shoved it into my hands and ordered me to sign.

What wasn't considered was that I could read it. The documents given to me were messages to Mrs Ascott, Roberts wife, and my parents. A detailed confession of my murdering Robin Ascott.

"SIGN!" barked the guard impatiently, and he struck me hard across my cheekbone splitting it in two with the back of his bare brutal hand and bringing me a new searing agony as I felt my cheek begin to throb.

Ascott stood in the corner still partially concealed by the shadows, but clearly, the guard could not see what I could see. I did not hesitate any longer. I thought perhaps this was what Ascott wanted. Maybe by my taking some of the blame then he would rest in peace, I certainly did not want him to follow me to the gallows and into what I wasn't sure was waiting for me in the afterlife.

So, I signed it.

Ascott lingered with me practically until I went to my death three days later. His focus on me never wavered once, and I became strangely used to his presence.

On the evening before I was executed, I declared how I was regretful for his untimely death and finally acknowledged that Harry James had deceived me. I was to swing for the crime that he committed.

I begged him for forgiveness and to allow me peace if he might.

I spoke to God and pleaded him to protect my parents and to permit them peace. I hoped with every last will in my body that they would recognise the handwriting in the letter was not my own and know somehow that I had been forced to confess.

Ascott's ghostly apparition faded gradually until

all that was left behind was the squalid concrete wall once more. I was not sorry to see him leave and felt an overwhelming sense of composure after that.

I went to my death absolved of liability. Justice would be done by Ascott's ghost, for that I was confident.

My own suffering was over, and I had to hope now that Harry James' was just about to begin.

Evening Express 23rd August 1898
MARSHAM MURDER
Confession of the Crime by Lewellyn! Condemned Man Writes to Mrs. Ascott.
All doubt, if any existed, that Lewellyn, the man at present awaiting his execution in Swansea Gaol, was guilty of shooting Game- keeper Ascott at Marsham has been removed by a letter written by the condemned man to Mrs. Ascott, the woman made a widow by the crime. The letter is extremely brief, and reads as follows:
"H.M. Prison, Swansea. "Dear Mrs. Ascott, I want to say to you that I sympathise with you in the sorrow I caused you to be in. What I did I did in self-defence. I hope you will try to forgive me. I am praying for him. I have no ill-feeling for anyone in the world.
Yours truly. Aug. 17, 1898.
LEWELLYN."

Though the letter is dated on Wednesday last, Mrs. Ascott did not receive it till Monday. The cause of the delay is easily supplied. The governor of the Swansea, Gaol, to whom the letter was handed in the first instance, did not know Mrs. Ascott's address. He sent it with other letters to Inspector Rutter of Maesteg who, it will be remembered, took a very active part in bringing the charge home to the accused.

Inspector Rutter in turn sent on the letter to Mr. Stubbs, the head gamekeeper on the Marsham Estate, and he delivered it in person to Mrs. Ascott on Monday morning.

The letter, while admitting the writer's guilt, made an insinuation which was not at all justified by the evidence given at the trial.

The sentence referred to is that in which Lewellyn gives as an excuse for the murder that he only acted in self-defence. The fact that Ascott was unarmed and that Lewellyn carried a gun, together with the facts that a wall lay between the two men from the time they came within speaking distance of each other, and that Lewellyn bore no mark of injury, all prove that any necessity for the deed from a motive of self-defence was purely imaginary on Lewellyn's part. The rest of the letter is plain, with, perhaps, the exception of the sentence, "I am praying for him," and goes to show that the condemned man is satisfied of the justice of the sentence passed upon him, is sorry for the woman whom he berefts of a husband, and intends, in the short time left doing all he can to prepare himself for his end.

PREPARING FOR THE EXECUTION. The prison authorities have given directions for the preparation of the scaffold for the execution of Joe Lewellyn, the Marsham murderer. The work will commence to-day (Tuesday). The execution will take place in the wheel-house, and the same "well" will be utilised. The only work, therefore, will be the overhauling of the cross bar and its supports, and the adaptation of a new mode of suspending the rope from the bar.

South Wales Daily News
26th August 1898

In an interview with Harry James of Maesteg, our representative learned that whilst Lewellyn was lodging in his house, extending over a period of 18 months, the latter would very frequently talk loudly in his sleep. Asked as to what Lewellyn used to talk about, Mr James replied, he used to fancy he was in India or Egypt soldiering.
When we asked him in the morning what he had been talking about he never appeared to know anything of it. Mrs James added that when in drink Lewellyn was very violent, and her husband had had to turn him out of the house. She further stated that after

a drinking bout Lewellyn would sometimes sit in a chair and prick himself about the hands badly with pins.

EVENING EXPRESS "29th August 1898
Our Llanelly interviewed the parents of the convict Lewellyn.

It is understood that his parents have decided that they cannot bear the ordeal of seeing him before his fate.
The mother, poor thing, who had been listening intently to the conversation, and with tears trickling down her cheeks, claimed frantically, "My boy would have never have done such a thing. He never killed the keeper." She then sobbed bitterly.
"A rumour is in circulation that your son did not confess to the crime?"
"I don't believe he himself has written a confession, although his signature is attached to the letter we received on Monday. The letter has not yet been out of my possession, and what has appeared in the newspapers is not exactly correct. Here it is..." he went on, as he handed me the important statement, "I have my doubts about the genuineness of the hand- writing," he added. The following is a copy of the letter: -

"Her Majesty's Prison, Swansea.
August 17, 1893.

Dear Father and Mother, Sisters, and all. I send my love to you all. I want to thank you for all you have done for me, and to say how sorry I am for the trouble I have given you.

I don't feel as if I was in prison at all. I am treated well and more like a gentleman than a prisoner. The Rev. D. Prosser and the Rev. Spencer James are doing their best; come in once a day both of them. About coming to see me, do as you think best. I am willing to see you if you wish. What I did was done in self-defence—he had a very big stick lifted up. I asked him to stop but he was quite near me when I saw him first. If he had stopped I would have given him my name, but he came straight on. I said, 'Stop!' with my gun raised. He said, Don't fire.' I said, I will if you don't stop.' I had nothing else to defend myself with, only my gun. It did not hinder him a bit, all that was said passed in less than a minute. I am asking pardon of God, and am in quite a different state from what I was when I came in. I am sending to the Ascotts' to speak of my sorrow for what I have done. My love once again to you all. I leave you in God's hands. Your affectionate son, JOE LEWELLYN . "

I wish this letter, brought by the Rev. Spencer James, to be given to Mr. P. T. Evans, for him to translate in Welsh to my father and mother," "So, it is not in your son's handwriting?". The signature, date, and postscript are certainly written by Joe Lewellyn." I observed, after examining the prison notepaper. "But my son is an excellent writer, and I don't understand what reason any official of the prison had to write a confession and then ask my son to sign it. Besides, the letter is dated August 17, while the postmark on the envelope is the 20th.

Authors Note

First, a huge THANK YOU my collection of short stories. They are availbale on kindle but only this paperback has the extra story of The Gamekeeper.

As a writer and researcher of the paranormal, Welsh folklore and dark history, my evolution from writing nonfiction articles for my blog and paranormal magazines and newspapers over to fiction has been a fascinating and thrilling journey.

My love for Wales I hope shines through in my stories, along with my dark fascination with the gothic era, where all the best ghost stories began.

My inspiration has always been real-life. I have a passion for discovering the long-forgotten articles of death, suicide, murder and ghostly goings on in Wales, found buried in news archives.

I have spent literally hours researching stories that capture my imagination. Using my artistic license, characters like Ellie, Florence and Dylan come to life, but they were all sparked by real life events. I hope you enjoy my imaginary recreation of the stories behind the stories.

If you did enjoy this book (and there is more to come!) I would really appreciate a review!

You can also read more of my work and my non – fictional research on my website
www.redragontales.com

Please do like my Author's page on Facebook here
www.facebook.com/walesparanormalwriter/

And follow me on Twitter here
twitter.com/MsClaireBarrand

About the Author

Claire Barrand is a writer and researcher of Welsh supernatural, ghosts and folklore from Abergavenny South Wales UK. Raised in an antique shop as a child, Claire had paranormal experiences from an early age and once managed a haunted pub in Bristol.

Now, a popular writer for various publications such as Spooky Isles and Haunted Magazine as well as her own blog, 'Red Dragon Tales', Claire also activly investigates the paranormal around the UK. Having investigated haunted locations with various famous paranormal investigators like Barry Fitzgerald, Barri Ghai, Jeff Belanger and John Zaffis, Claire puts her spooky experiences to good use in both her fiction and non-fiction writing.

Claire has been a spokesperson at U.K Paracons, as well as on radio and T.V. A a mother of four, and a lover of animals, happiness for this author is walking the dogs in the Welsh mountains and coming home to a cosy house filled with cats, guinea pigs, books, and pizza.

Printed in Poland
by Amazon Fulfillment
Poland Sp. z o.o., Wrocław